Lessons from the Heart

LESSONS from the HEART

♥

CHARLENE BOWEN

AVALON BOOKS
THOMAS BOUREGY AND COMPANY, INC.
401 LAFAYETTE STREET
NEW YORK, NEW YORK 10003

PRINTED IN THE UNITED STATES OF AMERICA
ON ACID-FREE PAPER
BY HADDON CRAFTSMEN, SCRANTON, PENNSYLVANIA

Rich—
Thanks for coming up with some really creative ideas

Chapter One

A frown creased Ashley Kendall's brow as her concentration was interrupted by a clamor outside her office. Ordinarily the din from the playground was simply background noise, but instinct told her this was more than the usual schoolyard hubbub. Her work as a counselor here at Soundview Academy—so named because its location afforded a magnificent view of western Washington's Puget Sound—had given her a sixth sense about these things.

With a distracted air, she ran a hand through her close-cropped dark curls. Turning her attention from the paperwork on her desk, she swiveled her chair around so it was facing the window and scanned the grounds until she located the source of the commotion.

A worried expression clouding her dark-fringed blue eyes, she studied the small knot of boys clustered together in one corner of the playground. They were Up To Something, there was no doubt about it. *I might have known*, she thought as she recognized the slightly built figure in the center of the group. Lately, whenever there was any kind of mischief afoot, Brandon Shepard

1

seemed to be the ringleader. For instance, just last week there was that firecracker incident in the library.

Ashley was getting up to go outside and investigate when Harriet Freeman, the teacher who had playground duty this week, also noticed the little stir of activity. Ashley sat back down, confident that Harriet would handle the matter. A veteran of many years of working with children, the peppery, no-nonsense little woman was more than a match for anything her students could cook up.

Ashley watched the pantomime that was being played out before her as Harriet approached the group. Although the other boys averted their eyes guiltily, Brandon's expression, beneath the shock of light-brown hair that fell over his forehead, was one of complete innocence.

Harriet was apparently asking him something, and Ashley could see him shaking his head. As the teacher persisted, he reluctantly withdrew his hands from behind his back and held out something. From this distance Ashley couldn't quite make out what it was. That was probably just as well, she thought with a shudder, recalling the episode with the mouse. Poor Miss Hubbard had almost fainted when she'd opened the top drawer of her desk and discovered the furry creature looking up at her curiously.

In the few months the three Shepard children had been students here at Soundview—ever since their parents had died in a car accident and they had become wards of an unmarried uncle—Brandon had gained quite a reputation. Academically he was above average. Although all his teachers agreed he was one of the brightest students in the school, his escapades kept him continually in hot water.

Ashley had had several sessions with him to discuss his conduct, and each one had left her feeling frustrated and ineffectual. The boy was cheerfully indifferent to her efforts to explain to him why certain aspects of his behavior were simply not acceptable.

"Brandon, when you're tempted to do something you know will get you into trouble, don't you ever stop to think about the consequences?" she asked in one of their counseling sessions.

He shrugged one shoulder in a classic gesture of unconcern.

Ashley tried another approach. "What does your uncle have to say about some of the things you do?"

Brandon grinned engagingly. "Uncle Mike says I'll be the death of him. He says he doesn't know what he's going to do about me."

From Brandon's attitude Ashley couldn't help wondering if Mr. Shepard was of the "boys will be boys" school of thought concerning his nephew's antics. Maybe he was even a little proud of Brandon's escapades. Or could it be that he was so involved in his own interests that he simply didn't care?

Ashley suppressed an impulse to voice her opinion of a guardian who had so little sense of responsibility. "I'm going to give you a note to take home to your uncle, asking him to come in for a conference. I've already sent several home with you, and I haven't received any answer. Are you *sure* you're giving these notes to him?"

"Oh, yes, ma'am," Brandon assured her.

Although his expression was as guileless as a baby's, Ashley couldn't help wondering if she was being taken in by a nine-year-old con artist.

If Brandon was the despair of the entire staff, at least his sisters were no problem, Ashley reflected. There was ten-year-old Sara, with her long, brown hair that fell halfway down her back, her grave, quiet manner, and her appealing air of maturity. Always helpful and eager to please, the little girl was a teacher's delight. If there was occasionally a look of sadness in her serious gray eyes—well, that was understandable.

And thoughts of six-year-old Jillian brought to mind ringlets, dimples, and a sunny disposition. With the resilience of the very young, she seemed to be making what could be considered "a good adjustment."

Of the three Shepard children, Brandon was the only one who presented any real cause for concern. Ashley felt certain she could find a way to divert his energy and lively imagination into more appropriate channels if she had the cooperation of his uncle. The policy here at Soundview was that the faculty worked in partnership with the student's parents—or guardian, in this case. So far, however, Mr. Shepard had ignored all her attempts to contact him. He apparently felt that once he'd enrolled his charges in one of Tacoma's most expensive and prestigious private schools, his obligation toward them was finished.

Well, it didn't work that way, she thought angrily. Soundview, which was noted for combining progressive methods of education with traditional values, usually had a long waiting list. He'd been fortunate to get them in at all. Now it was up to him to do his part.

Glancing out the window again, Ashley saw that the group of boys at the far end of the playground was dispersing. As she caught sight of Harriet heading toward her, she left her office and stepped out the side door of the building. "What was it this time?" she asked, intercepting the teacher.

Harriet rolled her eyes skyward, as though petitioning the heavens for strength. "The boys found a little garter snake, and Brandon had some creative ideas for what they could do with it. One involved the girls' rest room, I believe. I convinced them to turn it loose in the bushes."

"I don't think he means to get into trouble," Ashley commented thoughtfully. "He just has too much misdirected energy."

"That's what I have to remind myself regularly," Harriet said with a rueful smile. "It's the only thing that keeps me from wanting to strangle him."

The twinkle in her eye softened her blunt words. Ashley knew that beneath her caustic manner the teacher had a real affection for every one of her students—even Brandon.

Ashley laughed. "We're supposed to be the professionals. Between us, we ought to be able to handle one overactive nine-year-old kid."

"It would help a lot if we had some support from his uncle," Harriet said, echoing Ashley's own thoughts. "Have you been able to get in touch with the elusive Mr. Shepard?"

Ashley shook her head. "I sent a couple of notes home with Brandon, but I didn't get any reply. I even tried calling his work number, but I was always told he was 'unavailable,' and he's never returned my calls.''

''Hmm.'' Harriet's expression was thoughtful. ''I wonder if he's extremely busy or just not interested in Brandon's welfare. What does he do for a living?''

''According to Brandon's records, his uncle is an aerospace engineer out at Flint Aircraft,'' Ashley replied, referring to the aircraft manufacturing plant that contributed heavily to the area's economy. ''I realize it's wrong to judge a person without having all the facts, but I think I know the type—a slide rule in his pocket and his head full of mathematical equations. He's probably too involved in designing airplanes to even be aware that Brandon might have behavior problems.''

''So now what?'' Harriet asked. ''Not a week goes by that Brandon doesn't stir up some kind of trouble. And the other boys always go along with his ideas. *Something* has to be done about his behavior before he blows up the school or drives the entire faculty into a mental institution. And the staff can't do it alone. We need his uncle's support.''

''Oh, I'm not giving up.'' The discussion had given Ashley a renewed determination. ''If 'Uncle Mike' won't answer my notes or phone calls, I'll just have to pay him a visit. I think I'll drop in on the Shepard household this weekend. The school does encourage home visits, you know. Late Saturday morning would be a good time. People are usually home then. . . .'' Her words trailed off.

''Something wrong?'' Harriet asked.

''I just remembered—I promised Stewart I'd meet

him for lunch this Saturday and then go along to help him choose his new car." An expression of annoyance marred Ashley's features. Looking at cars with Stewart seemed a waste of a perfectly good Saturday. She'd tried to put him off by protesting that she didn't know enough about cars to offer a knowledgeable opinion, but—as usual—Stewart had brushed aside her objections. "I'll just have to call on Mr. Shepard first and go right from there to the restaurant."

"That's a sure sign that things are getting pretty serious, isn't it?" Harriet's tone was elaborately casual. "When a man asks you to help him pick out a car. . . ."

"Oh, Harriet—" Ashley began, but then she noticed the twinkle in the older woman's eye. Harriet was teasing her, of course. "I tried to get out of it, but Stewart can be—ah—very insistent."

"Well, all I can say is, you'd better be careful," Harriet cautioned. "Helping a man decide on a car is just a step away from choosing a silver pattern together."

Ashley shot a look at her friend. Harriet had such a dry sense of humor, it was sometimes hard to tell whether or not she was joking. And even if she *was*, her words evoked a little pang of apprehension in Ashley.

Somehow Ashley had become more involved with Stewart than she'd ever intended to. In fact, lately he'd been hinting that his plans for the future included her, and the idea filled her with dismay.

She was aware that many women would be pleased and flattered to have captured the interest of someone like Stewart Lattimer. Tall and blond, with an air of self-assurance, he was undeniably attractive. And there was no doubt he would go far. Already he was making a name for himself in financial circles as an investment broker.

And, of course, he was the type who would expect to have all the symbols of his success: the right clothes, the right car. The right wife. . . .

There went that little stab of uneasiness again. It wasn't just that, at twenty-eight, with her career now firmly established, Ashley was perfectly content with her single state. After several months of dating Stewart, she had realized their goals and values were worlds apart.

If Harriet caught the resigned sigh Ashley was unable to suppress, she refrained from comment. "So you're planning to beard the lion in his den?" she asked, returning to their earlier topic of conversation. "Have you ever met Mr. Shepard?"

"No, I wasn't here when he came in to enroll the children, and he never shows up for any school functions. He wasn't here for Parents' Night, or our track meet, or the spring program. It's time someone reminded him that those kids are his responsibility."

"Go for it!" Harriet raised a clenched fist in a gesture of encouragement.

Ashley flashed her a grin. "Uncle Mike, here I come!"

Just then the bell rang, signaling the end of recess. "I'd better get back to my classroom before my students get there. There's no telling what havoc the little darlings will wreak with Brandon as their ringleader,'' Harriet said.

Ashley wasn't shocked by her friend's words. She was aware that in spite of Harriet's outrageous comments, she was a caring, dedicated teacher. Although she threatened regularly to give up teaching and get into a less stressful line of work—like sword swallowing, perhaps—Ashley knew that Harriet could no sooner stop working with children than she could stop breathing. Humor was her method of dealing with some of the pressures of her job. It seemed to be effective, because she was liked and respected by all the students, as well as their parents and her coworkers.

"I'm not kidding,'' Harriet insisted, noting Ashley's amused expression. "If those kids are left unattended for long, they could have Mr. Applegate tied to a stake and be doing a war dance around him.''

Ashley couldn't suppress a giggle over the mental picture of their very dignified principal in such a predicament.

That evening, as Ashley tidied her kitchen after dinner, Harriet's words about Stewart kept coming back to her. Had there been a veiled warning behind the teasing comments? Harriet was perceptive enough to have sensed that Ashley was uncomfortable with the direction her relationship with Stewart was taking.

There was no doubt about it, she was just going to have to find a way to extricate herself from what was definitely becoming a sticky situation. Ordinarily she was an advocate of the direct approach, but she had a feeling that wouldn't work in this instance.

"I'll have to ease out of this thing gradually," she said to her marmalade-colored cat, Bridget, who was winding companionably around her ankles. "I guess I'm stuck with Stewart for this Saturday—I did promise I'd go with him—but after that, every time he calls and wants to see me, I'll just tell him I'm 'busy.' Eventually he'll get the message—I hope."

At the note of uncertainty in Ashley's voice, Bridget sat down and looked up at her mistress through half-closed eyes.

"Okay, I know it's the coward's way out," Ashley went on defensively as she loaded the dishwasher, "but sometimes it isn't easy to get through to Stewart. I couldn't even tell him I wasn't interested in going to look at cars with him and make it stick."

Bridget lifted a dainty paw and began to wash her face.

"Oh, you're no help." Ashley closed the door to the dishwasher and pushed the START button. Scooping up the cat, she went into the living room and sank down into her favorite chair. "What I need is advice."

Bridget emitted a noncommittal *meow*.

"You're absolutely right," Ashley said resolutely. "I'll just have to be firm. Polite but firm. That's the ticket."

Bridget curled up into her favorite nap position, as if to say, *Thank goodness we've got THAT settled.*

Ashley maneuvered her compact car next to the curb and examined the large split-level home located on a quiet cul-de-sac. With its weathered stone front and wide plate-glass windows, it was a comfortable blend of traditional and contemporary styling. Whatever else she thought about Mike Shepard, she had to admit he had good taste in houses.

She was surprised at the little red sports car in the driveway. In keeping with the picture she'd formed of "Uncle Mike," she supposed she'd been expecting something like a businesslike sedan. That certainly knocked holes in her preconceived theory that he was some ivory-tower intellectual only interested in his work. If the sports car was any indication, he was more likely a playboy type, in which case he was probably even less concerned about his young charges than she'd thought. Having three children thrust on him "cramped his style," no doubt.

What *was* it with men and their cars, anyway? The thought came to her as she recalled the big production Stewart was making out of finding just the right car to enhance his "image."

As she started up the steps to the front door, a little of her confidence began to desert her. What if Mr. Shepard didn't take kindly to her attempts to be helpful? What if he told her politely—or even *not* so politely—to "butt out"?

Wasn't Stewart always telling her she shouldn't get so involved in other people's business? Perhaps—in this instance, at least—he was right. For just a second or two she was almost tempted to get back into her car and drive away, but she caught herself just in time. What right did Stewart have to dictate how she should manage her affairs?

Besides, she owed this to Brandon, she reminded herself. If she was going to help the child learn to curb some of his more foolhardy impulses before he got himself into serious trouble, she needed his uncle's support. Squaring her shoulders and lifting her chin a fraction of an inch, she continued up the walk. She straightened the jacket of her trim, beige linen suit, carefully chosen to convey an image of competence and authority.

She was just about to ring the doorbell when a high-pitched shriek cut through the stillness. Ashley's hand froze in midair, an icy fear coursing through her. That was the scream of a frightened or injured child. She took several deep breaths, waiting for the rush of adrenaline that was pumping through her veins to subside. As she tried to make up her mind what course of action to take, another cry rang out.

Determinedly she jabbed the doorbell. ''Come on— I know somebody's in there,'' she muttered under her breath. There were muffled cries coming from inside, along with a bumping noise, as if something had fallen or been thrown.

In the back of her mind she could almost hear Stewart asking, ''Why didn't you just drive to the nearest phone and call the police?'' It occurred to her that that might be good advice. For all she knew, she could be walking in on an ax murder.

But it sounded as if somebody in there needed help. She couldn't just turn around and *leave*. Frantically she pressed the doorbell a second time.

It's about time, Mike thought as he jerked the door open impatiently. He stuck his head outside, and his glance went past the young woman on his doorstep to survey the area in front of the house, before returning to the petite brunette standing before him. Whatever she was selling, he didn't want any. He had enough to handle right now without being bothered by salespeople.

Ashley found herself confronted by a young man— early thirties, she would have guessed—clad in denim cutoffs, a tank top, and sandals. Although he was so tall he towered over her, the thought *He doesn't look like an ax murderer* flashed through her mind—even though she realized she had no idea of how an ax murderer looked. In spite of the scowl that marred his craggily handsome face, he looked more harried than dangerous. His wealth of thick dark hair was tousled, and his deep-brown eyes, with their bushy brows, seemed to be looking right through her, as if he didn't see her at all.

And that definitely wasn't an ax he had in his hand. It was, of all things, a teddy bear. Her confused senses focused on the object. The beat-up toy had the effect of counteracting the sinister aspects of the situation— the screams and cries and the muffled banging and bumping. It had one button eye missing, its fur was worn completely away in spots, and one leg dangled by a few threads.

So this was Uncle Mike. If he was nothing like her image of an ax murderer, neither did he resemble her original mental picture of some overly brainy type with thick glasses and a perpetually preoccupied expression. This man was an out-and-out *hunk*, she realized, taking in his strong, firm jaw and sensitive mouth, his muscular shoulders that tapered down to a flat stomach and slim hips.

Good legs too. The thought popped into her mind without warning. She felt her cheeks redden. *Behave yourself, Ashley,* she scolded. *You're here to discuss the man's nephew, not to admire his legs.*

She forced her attention back to the reason for her visit. "Mr. Shepard?" she managed to get out.

Mike nodded impatiently. How did this woman know his name? he wondered. Had he made some kind of appointment with her and then forgotten about it—

No, she had to be from the agency. He suppressed a groan. What could they have been thinking of, sending him someone like this? He thought he'd made his requirements very clear, but she wasn't what he'd had in mind at all. He couldn't take time to be choosy just now, though. For the time being, she'd have to do.

A flash of anger shot through Ashley at the way he was scowling at her. What could she have done to offend him? It was possible, of course, that he knew why she was here and resented the interference, but even if that was the case, he could at least exhibit common courtesy.

"I'm Ms. Kendall—Ashley Kendall—"

"Never mind that," he interrupted curtly. "There'll be time enough for introductions later—"

His words were cut off by a crash from somewhere behind him. He glanced over his shoulder briefly; then, with a muttered "Excuse me," he dashed off in the direction of the disturbance, leaving her standing in the open doorway.

Chapter Two

"**M**r. Shepard?" Ashley called uncertainly when he didn't return. Although her every instinct told her to turn around and run, her conscience wouldn't allow her to do so without further investigation. Somebody could be hurt in there.

After a few moments of indecision, she stepped through the open door. She found herself in a roomy entryway, with a hall going off to one side and a wide double doorway directly in front of her that apparently led into the living room. From where she stood, she had a glimpse of thick, off-white carpeting. It was marred by a crisscross pattern of dark, dirty splotches, and almost past her line of vision were the remains of what appeared to have once been a lamp. Now it was nothing but a jumble of shattered pieces.

She could hear a child's—possibly Jillian's—sobs coming from the living room, and another voice that sounded like Sara's murmuring in low, soothing tones. What was going on here?

Just as Ashley took a tentative step forward for a closer look, something large and furry—and wet—burst through the wide doorway. As her startled mind

15

grasped that this was not the abominable snowman, but rather a very big dog, cries of "Catch him!" and "Don't let him get away!" rang out.

Instinctively she reached behind her and closed the front door. That avenue of freedom blocked, the dog looked around wildly, then changed direction and headed down the hallway.

With the slightly hysterical feeling that she had blundered into a Saturday-morning cartoon, Ashley gave chase. Had she taken time to consider the matter, she might have questioned the wisdom of attempting to subdue a large, frightened dog bent on escape. It wasn't until he skidded to a stop at the end of the passageway, his feet slipping on the uncarpeted floor, that it occurred to her to wonder, *What do I do now?*

Cornered, the dog turned to face her, almost tripping over his huge feet in the process. Was he going to try to get past her? Ashley wondered. And if he did, would she be able to stop him? More important, did she really *want* to?

Ashley eyed the animal warily. She didn't like the look in his eyes. A sudden chill ran through her as she sensed his intention. "Oh, no!" she cried, backing away. "Please don't—"

But it was too late. Planting his feet squarely on the floor to brace himself, he shook his massive body from head to tail, sending a spray of muddy water all over the walls, the floor—and Ashley.

Her mouth opened and closed several times, but the only sound she could utter was a little gasp. Her primary thought right then was to get as far out of the dog's range as possible, before he decided to shake himself again. As she turned to hurry down the hall, she skidded on a wet spot on the floor. One foot slipped out from under her, and she reached out wildly in a vain attempt to grab onto something. Her stomach swooped up into her throat as she felt herself falling.

Suddenly a pair of muscular arms came around her, and she found herself engulfed in a viselike hug. When she could gather her scattered wits together, she realized the side of her face was pressed against a firm, hard chest. She could hear a rhythmic thudding against her ear—or was that her own heartbeat? Suddenly she felt shaky. She couldn't understand how something as trivial as a near fall could cause this weakness in her limbs, but for a brief moment she had the feeling her legs might not support her. Instinctively she gave in to an urge to rest in that protective embrace for just a second.

The almost imperceptible tightening of those arms around her brought her to her senses abruptly. Taking a deep, calming breath, she twisted free.

The entire episode was over in seconds. Mike's startled senses barely had time to register that this person who had fallen into his arms was small and soft—and very feminine—before she sagged against him ever so slightly. She seemed as if she might be about to faint, and his hold on her automatically tightened. Then she was backing out of his embrace, leaving him with nothing but the lingering scent of her perfume and a vague, inexplicable sense of loss. It was just as well, his common sense told him as he forced his thoughts back into line. This was strictly a business arrangement. He certainly didn't need to make things any more complicated than they already were.

"Are you all right?" he asked as Ashley struggled to regain her equilibrium and her composure.

"I—I'm fine. I just. . . ." Her words trailed off as she raised her head and found herself looking into a pair of warm brown eyes. *They have gold flecks in them,* she thought irrelevantly.

The realization that Brandon had come up behind his uncle and was taking in this entire scene, his eyes wide with interest, brought her back to herself with a start. This would never do. She'd come here to have a professional discussion with Brandon's uncle, and practically the first thing she'd done was fall right into his arms. And now she was gazing into his eyes and stammering like a schoolgirl. She told herself her unexpected reaction was just because everything had happened so fast. She just needed a second or two to catch her breath and pull herself together.

It would be easier to organize her thoughts if Mike Shepard weren't standing so close. Even though he'd dropped his arms as soon as she'd managed to regain her balance, he was still near enough that she could feel the heat from his body.

She took a step backward. "I—ah—must have slipped on a wet spot. Thank you for keeping me from falling," she said, striving to keep her voice crisp and impersonal.

"No problem. As long as there's no real harm done. . . ."

No harm! Ashley thought. Couldn't he see what that stupid dog of his had done to her? She was a mess!

She could feel little trickles of water dripping down from her hair into her face. She gave a cry of dismay as she glanced down at her suit. It was spattered with drops of dirty water. She had planned to go directly from here to the restaurant to meet Stewart, but now she would have to go home and change first. She would be late, of course, and Stewart had a tendency to get a little testy when he was kept waiting.

"Hey, I'm sorry about that," Mike said. "You really should have worn something a little more practical, though."

His remark wiped away the last vestige of whatever emotion she'd felt during those few seconds in his arms. Just because he was overpoweringly attractive, that didn't give him the right to criticize her attire. And what was wrong with what she was wearing, anyway? What did the women of his acquaintance go around in—bib overalls? But before she could voice the angry retort that sprang to her lips, he turned to Brandon and ordered, "Go get a towel. And then take that dog out of here."

"But—"

"Do it now!" his uncle snapped.

The boy seemed about to say something else, then apparently thought better of it. Muttering under his breath, he turned and left. He was back shortly with a towel, which he handed to Ashley. As she dabbed at her hair, face, and clothes, Brandon looked up at his uncle, a worried expression on his small face. He was clearly bothered over something.

Mike frowned at the dog, who was dripping all over the floor. "I thought I told you to do something with that animal,'' he said to Brandon. ''You can put him in the basement until we figure out what to do about him. We can't let him run around the neighborhood loose.''

''But he'll get lonesome—''

His protests were effectively quelled by his uncle's stern look. Mike turned his attention back to Ashley. ''After you get yourself dried off, you can clean up the water on the walls and floor while I go see what I can do about the mess in the living room.''

Ashley's jaw dropped open in astonishment. Who did this guy think he was, ordering her to do his *housework*? But before she could let him know what she thought of his highhandedness, Brandon cut in with, ''Listen, Uncle Mike. I—um—I have to tell you something—''

''Do as I say before he causes any more trouble,'' his uncle snapped.

With a shrug and a resigned sigh, Brandon grabbed a handful of fur and tugged. The dog went with him willingly, his mouth hanging open in a doggy grin, as if he were enjoying all the excitement. Mike watched them go, then stalked off down the hallway himself.

Ashley stared after him. If he thought she was going to stay here and be a—a scullery maid, he certainly had another think coming! Her first impulse was to go after this overbearing man and give him a piece of her mind. As she was about to throw the towel down, however, she caught sight of the rivulets of dirty water trickling down the wallpaper. They were already starting to leave white spots on the polished floor. Instinctively her sense of neatness took over. Without intending to, she found herself wiping up the walls and floor.

Muttering under her breath, she wielded the towel with vicious motions, as if it were a weapon. The only reason she was doing this, she told herself, was to give herself a chance to cool off before confronting Mike Shepard. She needed the vigorous activity to vent the anger that was building up inside her. Otherwise she might say things she would later regret.

Just as she dried up the last bead of water, she was startled by a blast of noise that came on so suddenly, her heart slammed against her ribs. It could best be described as a cross between a buzz and a whistle, and it brought with it a sense of urgency, as if warning her of something she ought to do. But it was hard to think clearly with those shrill, penetrating tones ringing in her ears.

Then, mercifully, the noise stopped. Of course—it was a smoke detector, she realized as she gathered her thoughts together. A whiff of something burning sent a stab of alarm through her. Fortunately she wasn't far from the front door. But the children were in the house. She couldn't leave without making sure they were safely out.

She could hear excited voices coming from another room. Frantically she followed the sound, fearful that the children were trapped somewhere. Racing through the living room and dining room, she stopped short when she reached the kitchen.

Through a smoky haze she could see Mike and the three children staring glumly at a casserole dish on the counter, the contents of which were charred beyond recognition. A few wisps of smoke still emanated from it. She noticed that Jillian now had possession of the teddy bear and was clutching it protectively.

Brandon inspected the casserole. "Wow!" he said in awed tones. "It looks just like charcoal."

Ashley's curiosity got the better of her. "Wh-what *is* that?" she asked, approaching the counter for a closer look.

"It was supposed to be lunch," Mike replied. "With everything else that was going on around here, I just forgot it was in the oven."

"We're not gonna have to *eat* that, are we?" Brandon asked.

Before he could reply, a low, mournful howl rose up from somewhere in the lower part of the house.

"He's probably hungry too," Brandon commented.

"I guess we're stuck with that animal until I can locate his owner or have the pound come and pick him up," Mike grumbled.

At the mention of the pound, Brandon opened his mouth to protest but subsided after a pointed look from his uncle.

"I'd better run down to the store and pick up some dog food. Maybe that'll shut him up." Mike glanced at Ashley. "While I'm gone, see what you can rustle up for these kids to eat."

He was doing it again. Did he think she was some kind of genie who had appeared at his door solely to do his bidding? But Ashley held back her angry words as she realized that three pairs of eyes were looking at her expectantly. She was aware that all three children were capable of at least slapping together a peanut-butter sandwich and pouring a glass of milk.

Still, she hesitated, wondering if she ought to go off and leave them at the mercy of this man. Something violent had obviously taken place here today, judging from the screams and the broken lamp. Although the children didn't appear to have been actually mistreated or abused, she felt duty bound to stick around long enough to get a closer look at things.

"I—I'll see what I can do," she murmured.

Giving a brief nod, as if to indicate that was no less than he expected from her, Mike turned to leave.

With Sara showing her where things were kept, Ashley took stock of the kitchen supplies. *Perfect,* she thought, when she discovered pepperoni and cheese in the refrigerator and tomato sauce, oregano, and a container of pizza-crust mix in the cupboard. Pizza would keep her here long enough to size up the situation.

With Sara's help she soon had two pepperoni pizzas assembled. She was just sliding them into the oven when Jillian, who had been watching the proceedings silently, gave a long, shuddering sigh.

Ashley's heart went out to the little girl, who looked so sad. "What is it, honey?" she asked.

Without a word Jillian held out the teddy bear she'd been clutching. Her large, expressive blue eyes went to the leg that was about to fall off.

"Poor teddy," Ashley said sympathetically. "He seems to have been in an accident. Would you like me to fix him?"

Jillian nodded, not taking her eyes from Ashley's

face. "I'll go get a needle and thread," Sara volunteered.

With Jillian solemnly watching her every move, Ashley sewed the teddy bear's leg back on with careful, even stitches.

"His name's Woober," the little girl said.

"Woober. That's a nice name."

"It's really J. Worthington Bear," Sara explained. "But when Jilly was little, she pronounced it 'Woober,' and it stuck."

When Ashley tied the final knot and handed the toy back to Jillian, she was rewarded with a smile as radiant as a summer morning.

During this entire time, the howls from the basement had been permeating the air, gradually increasing in volume. By the time Mike Shepard returned with a bag of K-Nine Krunchies, Ashley was contemplating several methods of silencing the animal, none of which would have met with the approval of the SPCA.

She noted that Mike winced with each howl. His lips were set in a tight line, and his jaw was clenched as he filled a bowl with dog food and another with water.

The howls began to taper off shortly after he disappeared through a door that apparently led to the basement. By the time he returned, the house was blessedly quiet, Ashley had cleared away the remains of the charred casserole, and the children were seated at the table, contentedly munching pizza.

"Gosh, Miss Kendall, all this time I never knew you could cook," Brandon said, reaching for another slice.

Mike had gone to the cupboard to put away the bag of K-Nine Krunchies. At Brandon's words he turned around slowly. His glance darted from Brandon to Ashley and back again. "You kids already *know* Miss Kendall?"

"Sure," Brandon replied through a mouthful of pizza. "We see her almost every day—"

Fragmented thoughts whirled through Mike's mind as he digested this information. There was something vaguely familiar about the name Kendall, but he couldn't quite put his finger on it. Something was definitely out of kilter here, he realized. "I—ah—I take it you're not from the agency, then," he finally said.

The agency? The only thing that came to Ashley's mind was Central Intelligence Agency. But somehow the events that were taking place around here didn't quite fit in with her idea of a cloak-and-dagger operation. "I'm the counselor from Soundview Academy," she informed him.

Oh, boy, Mike thought. *Now you've really done it.* He should have realized the minute he set eyes on her that she wasn't the housekeeper he'd told the agency to send. He groaned inwardly as he recalled the way he'd been snapping orders at her. But it had been hard to think clearly with that blasted dog running around crashing into things and wrecking his house, and Jilly crying as if her heart were breaking.

"I hate to even imagine what you must be thinking about me," he said at last. "You see, I'd called the Domestic Service Agency and told them to send someone out right away. I just thought—" He broke off and glared at the children. ''Why didn't you kids tell me?''

''I tried to, Uncle Mike,'' Brandon reminded him virtuously, ''but you wouldn't listen.''

Mike summoned a smile. ''Actually, once I explain what's been happening around here, you're going to think the whole situation is hilarious—'' He broke off, noting Ashley's skeptical look. ''Well, maybe not exactly hilarious,'' he amended, ''but at least funny— Mildly amusing?'' he asked hopefully.

She continued to glare at him. *This better be good,* her expression said.

''That was Jilly screaming,'' he explained, ''because the dog ran off with her Woober—I guess I'd better start from the top. It all began when Brandon went to the park this morning to play and came home with the Hound of the Baskervilles. He insists the dog followed him.''

''He did—honest,'' Brandon put in. ''I kept telling him to go away, but he wouldn't.''

Mike paused to frown at him before going on with his story. ''When Brandon brought him home, my housekeeper, Mrs. Harper, hit the ceiling. She had been threatening to quit at least once a week, but this time I couldn't really blame her when practically the first thing the dog did was chew up her slippers.''

''He thought they were wild animals,'' Brandon put in. ''She wore those fuzzy blue kind. Anyway, she shouldn't have left her bedroom door open.''

''I guess the final straw was when Brandon gave him a bath with Mrs. Harper's bubble bath,'' Mike went on.

"She called him a filthy animal," Brandon explained, the picture of injured innocence. "I just thought if I cleaned him up, she'd like him better."

Mike ignored that. "She packed her things and left in such a hurry that she didn't even take time to take the casserole out of the oven."

With a martyred air Sara supplied the information that, "All of our housekeepers quit. One of them said she'd never seen a child like Brandon."

"Anyway, while I was calling the agency to have them send out another housekeeper, the dog got out of the bathroom, and we had to chase him through the house. That's how the lamp got broken—"

"He was still scared because of the way Mrs. Harper yelled at him," Brandon interrupted.

His uncle had the look of one who was struggling to hang on to his patience. "He didn't look very upset to me. He seemed to be having the time of his life. While we were chasing him, he got hold of Woober—Jilly's teddy bear, that is—and decided it made a great toy. That was what Jilly was screaming about. She's had Woober since—since—" He broke off. "Well, he's very important to her. I managed to rescue him, but, as you can see, he was wounded in action. And—well, that's about where you came in. You know the rest."

His expression was as earnest as Brandon's as he recounted the events of the morning.

Ashley wasn't sure what to say. Even though she was still smarting over the way he had ordered her around, she had to admit, the story *must* be true. It was too fantastic to have been made up. "That's—

ah—quite a tale, Mr. Shepard,'' she managed to get out.

He grinned, obviously relieved that she seemed to believe him. Why, he didn't seem like such a villain, after all, when he smiled that way, Ashley thought. Apparently nothing sinister had gone on here. And it *was* kind of funny.

"Hey, under the circumstances I think you could call me Mike, couldn't you? I mean, there's no need to stand on ceremony after you've mopped a man's floor and made pepperoni pizza for his kids—'' He broke off with a puzzled frown. "I know you didn't drop by just because you heard things were getting a little out of hand here and I needed some help. If you don't mind my asking, just what *are* you doing here?''

In all the confusion, Ashley's original reason for coming here had slipped her mind. Now her resentment returned as she recalled the unanswered notes, the phone calls he hadn't bothered to return. "I've been trying to contact you to ask you to come to the school for a conference.''

"A conference?''

Apparently he was unfamiliar with the concept of parent-faculty conferences. "There are certain aspects of Brandon's behavior that we have to discuss—'' She broke off, aware that Brandon was watching her warily at the mention of his name. "It's the policy at Soundview for faculty members to meet with the parents of our students at regular intervals.''

All at once understanding dawned. "Brandon's been giving you trouble, huh.'' It was a statement, not a question.

Ashley was caught off guard. Because she hadn't received any replies to her notes or phone calls, she had assumed that he was too involved in his own concerns to even notice that Brandon had a behavior problem. But after this morning's experience, she realized he was probably all too aware of the boy's talent for getting into trouble.

"I'm sorry I had to bother you at home, Mr. Shepard—"

"Mike," he corrected her.

"Mike," she amended automatically, "but the notes I sent home with Brandon were never answered."

"I don't recall getting any—" He broke off and looked over at Brandon, who seemed to have become very interested in gazing out the window. "What happened to those notes?"

Brandon dragged his attention away from the window. "I brought them home, just like I was supposed to."

"But you didn't *give* them to me. Now what did you do with them?" His tone indicated that the time for evasion was past and he wanted a straight answer.

"I—uh—I put them in the desk in the study."

"Brandon, there are about a million pieces of paper in that desk. Did you even *mention* to me that you had put them there?"

Brandon nodded virtuously.

"And what was I doing when you told me?" Mike's tenuous grip on his patience was obviously about to give way.

"Well"—Brandon's brow furrowed in concentration—"once you were trying to talk Mrs. Harper out

of quitting. You offered her a raise,'' he recalled help-
fully. ''And another time you were busy at your work-
table. And once—''

''Never mind,'' Mike barked. ''I get the idea. We'll
have a serious discussion about those notes later,'' he
said in a tone that spoke volumes.

He turned his attention back to Ashley. ''Look, I'm
really sorry about this.''

The whole thing sounded plausible, Ashley thought,
giving Mr. Shepard—*Mike*—the benefit of the doubt.
It wouldn't be the first time a note she'd given a student
hadn't made it home. But all the blame couldn't be
laid on Brandon. ''I called your work number several
times and left word for you to get in touch with me.''

Mike slapped a palm against his forehead. ''Kendall
... Kendall ...'' he muttered. ''I remember now. I
was told that a Ms. Kendall had been trying to reach
me. I meant to return your calls, but—well, things
have been kind of hectic at work. We're having some
problems with this new design— But never mind that.
How about Monday morning?''

''For the conference? Why, I—I suppose.''

''Fine. I'll be in your office at nine o'clock. And I
really am sorry you had to make a personal visit just to
set up an appointment, but at least I know my kids are in
good hands if you're that interested in their welfare.
And mopping up the floor and fixing lunch was really
going above and beyond the call of duty—''

Lunch. The word set off an alarm in the back of her
mind. She was supposed to have met Stewart for lunch.
A glance at her watch confirmed that she was late.
Even though she'd made the decision to stop seeing

him, she couldn't, in good conscience, simply leave him sitting there waiting for her to show up.

"Is something wrong?" Mike asked, noting her expression of dismay.

"Yes—no—I mean, may I use your phone?"

"Certainly. Help yourself—"

Without waiting for him to finish, she rushed to the living room, where she had noticed a telephone on an end table. As she punched out the number of the restaurant and asked to have Stewart paged, she could picture him becoming more and more impatient when she didn't show up on schedule.

"Yes?"

The clipped monosyllable confirmed that he was upset. "Stewart . . ." she began.

"Ashley? Where are you? You were supposed to have been here twenty minutes ago. It's not like you to be late."

She was about to tell him she'd have to go home and change before she could meet him, but she didn't feel up to trying to explain why. "Something came up. I'm afraid I won't be able to make it."

"But the BMW salesman is expecting us in a little while."

In her mind Ashley could see his handsome face drawn into a disapproving frown. She was on the verge of telling him how sorry she was, but, in all honesty, she couldn't work up any regret at having been granted this reprieve.

"Ashley, are you still there?"

"Yes, of course." She forced her thoughts back to

the matter at hand. "You'd better go ahead without me."

"If you can't make it, I suppose I have no choice. Look, why don't I pick you up for dinner this evening? There's something I want to talk to you about."

Ashley hesitated. This would be the perfect opportunity to start putting her new strategy— of easing out of her relationship with Stewart—into practice. All she had to do was tell him she had other plans.

But before she could get the words out, he said, "I'll pick you up at seven." He hung up before she could protest.

Well, so much for polite but firm, she thought wryly.

When she returned to the kitchen, Mike was seated at the table with the children. He jumped up and pulled out a chair for her. "We saved some pizza for you."

Her brief, unsatisfactory conversation with Stewart had left her with such a feeling of frustration, she was afraid that if she tried to eat anything, it would sit in her stomach like a lump of lead. "Thank you, but I really have to be going," she said.

The tense note in her voice caused Mike to glance at her curiously, but he didn't press the issue. "I'll see you Monday morning, then."

Chapter Three

Stewart put his knife and fork down and looked across the table at Ashley. His features were set in an expression of irritation.

"Now, let me see if I have this straight. You went to this man's house and helped capture his dog, which was on some sort of rampage? Good heavens, Ashley, the beast could have turned on you."

"It—it wasn't his dog. It was a stray. And he wasn't really on a rampage—he was just frightened."

"Then you cleaned up after the dog, fixed lunch for the children, and repaired the little girl's—what did you say she called it?"

"Her—ah—Woober. It's kind of a pet name for a teddy bear she's very attached to. It's. . . ." She was going to explain that Woober was short for J. Worthington Bear, but instinct told her Stewart wouldn't be at all interested in that fact.

"Her 'Woober,' " Stewart echoed dryly. "And this man *allowed* you to do all this?"

"I told you, he thought I was the housekeeper."

"I see." Stewart's tone made it clear that he saw more than a simple misunderstanding in the situation.

It was obvious he considered it highly unlikely she could be mistaken for a housekeeper. "And it never occurred to you to set him straight?"

"There wasn't any opportunity. In all the confusion. . . ." Her voice trailed off as she realized he was putting her on the defensive again. Darn it, why did she allow him to do that?

Stewart shook his head. "I've told you before, you need to learn to assert yourself."

"But my job—"

"Being an unpaid servant for some man who can't manage his household is *not* part of your job. You have to stop letting people take advantage of you."

Ashley bit off a sharp reply. Since she'd already made up her mind to end their relationship, anyway, she saw no point in arguing with him. "Did you get everything settled about the car?" she asked in an attempt to change the subject. Then, noting the way his jaw tightened, she wished she hadn't brought it up.

"Yes, I take delivery in a few weeks. But I was counting on your input on such matters as colors and upholstery styles." His clipped tones clearly indicated he was still annoyed.

Suddenly Ashley felt she'd had about all she could take. "Oh, for Pete's sake!" she burst out, with such vehemence that several other diners glanced at them curiously. "I explained what happened," she went on in a lower voice. "I couldn't just walk out until I found out if those children were in some kind of trouble."

"But they weren't. There was nothing going on that your Mr. Shepard couldn't have handled—"

"He's not *my* Mr. Shepard!" Ashley snapped. "And

what if there really had been a fire and I had to help get the children out? Or if I'd encountered an accident while I was driving here and had to stop and give aid? Should I have said, 'I'm sorry, I can't help you now. I have to go help someone decide what kind of upholstery he wants in his new BMW'?''

He seemed a little taken aback by her tirade, as if he realized he'd gone too far. "I'm sorry, Ashley," he apologized in a placating tone. "Maybe I did overreact just a little. It's just that—well, maybe it's selfish of me, but I don't like sharing you with a lot of other people. If we're going to have a future together—"

"Future together?" she choked. A churning sensation started up in her stomach as she realized what he was working up to.

He started to reach across the table to take her hand, but she forestalled the contact by averting her glance and concentrating on the food on her plate. When she stole a quick look at him, she saw him pause uncertainly, then withdraw his hand.

He cleared his throat. "Ashley, we've been seeing each other several months now. I think it's time—" Their waiter approached with a coffee decanter, but Stewart waved him away with an impatient gesture. "I think it's time we talked about making our relationship permanent."

Oh, no, Ashley thought in panic. She found herself fervently hoping for some sort of distraction—maybe a waiter dropping a tray of dishes, or a fire in the kitchen. Not a serious fire, of course—just one large enough to create a diversion.

"Ashley, you must know by now how I feel about you—"

"Lattimer, old man. Whattaya say!"

A frown of annoyance crossed Stewart's face as a hearty male voice broke in on his words. When he glanced up, however, he forced his features into a semblance of a smile. "George Baker. It's—ah—good to see you," he said to the middle-aged man who had stopped at their table.

"Great to see you too. When I spotted you here, I told Margaret"—he indicated the pleasant-looking woman at his side—"we had to come over and say hello. Oh, I'd like you to meet my wife. Margaret, you've heard me mention Stewart Lattimer—he handles all my investments—and—" He looked at Ashley expectantly.

"Ashley Kendall," Stewart supplied. Somewhat reluctantly he got to his feet. "Ashley—George and Margaret Baker. George is a client of mine."

After a little stir of handshakes and murmured acknowledgments, Baker said, "I'm sure glad I ran into you, Lattimer. I'm onto a couple of deals that sound pretty good, but I wanted to run them by you first."

"Now, George," Mrs. Baker chided, "let these people finish their dinner. This is no time to talk business."

Baker blinked in surprise, as if it hadn't occurred to him that they might be intruding. "Hey, I'm not interrupting anything, am I?"

Stewart shot Ashley a look that spoke volumes. She'd heard him mention Baker before, and she knew he was an important enough client that Stewart would want to give him his full attention. She felt the tension that had been building up inside her begin to dissipate as she realized this was the diversion she'd been hoping for. Trying to keep her relief from being too obvious, she indicated, with a barely perceptible nod, that it was all right.

She managed to keep her expression impassive as Stewart gave her an approving glance. He thought she was being supportive and understanding, of course— exactly the qualities he would expect in a wife.

"No, of course you're not interrupting anything," Stewart assured Baker, adopting a hearty tone. "We'd love to have you and your wife join us. Wouldn't we, Ashley?"

"Certainly," she replied with real sincerity. She felt as if she'd been granted a reprieve.

The waiter, who had been standing by waiting for further developments, hurried to pull out a chair for Mrs. Baker. She smiled apologetically as she seated herself and opened her menu.

For the next hour or so such terms as "stock options," "diversified portfolio," and "high-yield securities" were bandied about between Stewart and Baker. The two women had little in common, and conversation limped along as they tried to find some area of mutual interest. When Mrs. Baker made casual mention of a grandson, Ashley grabbed onto the comment as if it were a life raft and she were drowning.

"Oh, you have a grandchild?" she said, almost too brightly. Anything to break up those stretches of silence that were growing longer and more uncomfortable.

That was all the encouragement the older woman

needed. "Oh, my, yes. I have five." It didn't take her long to warm up to what was obviously her favorite topic, and in no time she was digging in her purse for pictures of her grandchildren and recounting tales of their antics. Ashley found that all she had to do was smile every now and then and make automatic responses at the appropriate times.

"And this is Chuckie," Mrs. Baker said, displaying a snapshot of a chubby toddler. "Isn't he a doll?"

"Yes, he's adorable," Ashley murmured, although the child looked to her very much like every other two-year-old. Her head was beginning to ache, and her facial muscles felt as if they were frozen into a permanent smile.

She didn't blame Mrs. Baker, of course. The woman was just trying to make the best of an uncomfortable situation. And Ashley reminded herself that spending an evening listening to a complete stranger tell about her grandchildren was preferable to fending off Stewart's marriage proposal. Under other circumstances Ashley probably would even have enjoyed hearing about the Baker grandchildren.

"And *smart*—" Mrs. Baker went on. "Let me tell you what he said the other day—"

"Hey, Maggie, we'd better get moving," Baker interrupted, glancing at his watch. "I guess I've taken up enough of your time," he said to Stewart. "We can continue this discussion in your office next week."

Once the Bakers were gone, Ashley was afraid Stewart might want to resume the proposal he'd started earlier. Maybe he sensed that the timing would definitely not be right just now, however, because he simply said, "We'd better be going too. It's getting late."

On the way home Stewart reached over and took her hand. She disengaged it on the pretext of looking at her watch.

"Ashley?"

She leaned her head against the back of the seat and closed her eyes. "Ummm?" she replied.

"I'm really sorry about the way the evening turned out. Of course, once Baker showed up, I didn't have much choice. I do a lot of business with him, so I couldn't just brush him aside."

"It's quite all right," she murmured. "Don't give it another thought."

"Would you like to stop someplace for a drink?"

"No, thank you." She had had more than enough of Stewart's company for one day.

For the rest of the ride home, Ashley responded to his attempts at conversation with brief monosyllables. Opening her eyes slightly, she stole a glance at him. It was obvious, from the set of his jaw, that he was annoyed. It occurred to her that he probably thought she was sulking because he had allowed his marriage proposal to be interrupted while he conferred with a client.

It was a relief when they finally reached Ashley's apartment. As she was digging her key out of her purse, Stewart said, "That discussion we were having before Baker showed up—we'll get back to that later." His voice held a meaningful note.

Not if I can help it, Ashley thought. She found the prospect so unnerving that she almost dropped her key.

She could tell, by the look in Stewart's eyes, that he meant to kiss her good night. With trembling fingers, she managed to get her door unlocked and slip inside before he could carry out his intention.

Bridget met her at the door. Rubbing her head against Ashley's ankles, she emitted a soft *meow*.

"Thank you for asking, but no, I didn't have a nice evening," Ashley replied, bending down to stroke Bridget's silky head. "As a matter of fact, I had a perfectly awful time."

Chapter Four

Ashley glanced at her watch. Almost nine o'clock. Mike Shepard would be here any minute. She started to take a quick peek in the mirror she kept in the top drawer of her desk, to give her hair a final pat. Then, catching herself, she slammed the drawer shut.

What was wrong with her, anyway? This was a parent-counselor conference, for heaven's sake—not a date. All that was expected of her, in the way of looks, was that she present a neat, well-groomed appearance.

Still, she couldn't deny that she'd chosen her outfit with special care this morning. She remembered that she'd spent a long time surveying her wardrobe. She'd finally settled on a slim skirt that emphasized her slender hips and a blouse in a shade that brought out the blue of her eyes.

Well, what was wrong with wanting to start off the week looking her best? she asked herself defensively. Didn't everyone need a little lift on Monday mornings? It had nothing to do with the fact that she had an appointment with Mike Shepard.

And right now she felt she was entitled to that lift. She'd had a miserable weekend. After her dinner with

Stewart Saturday evening, it had become alarmingly clear to her that she had a real problem. She had spent all day Sunday considering how she was going to extricate herself from this situation.

"Just easing out of the relationship gradually isn't going to do it," she'd lamented to Bridget. "I might as well admit it, he'll never get the hint. It just wouldn't occur to him that I'm simply not interested in him."

Bridget jumped up into her lap and gazed at her solemnly.

"My problem is that I'm too polite," Ashley went on. Bridget regarded her with an unblinking yellow stare. "Oh, all right, make that 'cowardly.' But, I swear, I never meant for things to go this far."

Purring, Bridget nuzzled Ashley's chin. "Yes, I love you too," Ashley murmured, absentmindedly caressing the small cat. "But that doesn't help me figure out how to get my message across to Stewart."

She fell silent as she considered her options. "I'll just have to get tough," she finally said, putting Bridget off her lap and getting up with an air of determination. "No more Ms. Nice Guy."

Bridget gave her a resentful look before turning her attention to smoothing her ruffled fur.

When Ashley finally fell asleep that night, after hours of tossing and turning, she had restless dreams in which she was trying to tell Stewart something very important, but she just couldn't seem to make him listen.

She'd awakened feeling frustrated and disoriented—and vaguely guilty, as if she'd brought this whole thing on herself. Reflecting on it now, she realized she was going to have to take some definite action before she got in any deeper than she already was.

Her thoughts were interrupted by a light tap, followed by the door opening. "I have a few minutes before class starts," Harriet said, sticking her head in. "I just thought I'd check in and find out how your visit with 'Uncle Mike' went."

"Oh, hi, Harriet. Come on in."

The teacher stepped inside and closed the door. "Well, what's he like? Did he take kindly to a personal visit, or did he get all hostile at the suggestion that *his* nephew might be a troublemaker?"

"It was an—an interesting visit."

"Interesting in what way?" Harriet prodded.

Ashley hadn't planned on going into the whole story until they had more time, but she realized that just "interesting" wasn't going to satisfy Harriet. "Well, as I was walking up to the front door, I heard these horrible screams coming from inside the house," she began. "I wanted to turn around and run away, but I thought somebody might be hurt and need my help. And then this man came to the door, but before I could introduce myself, there was a crash from somewhere behind him, and he took off and left me standing there. . . . Look, wouldn't you rather wait until lunchtime to hear the rest of this? I know you have to get to your classroom."

Harriet leaned against the door and folded her arms. "After hearing this much, wild horses couldn't drag me away," she declared.

Quickly Ashley went on to relate the "high points" of the visit: the wet, shaggy dog, the burned casserole, and the case of mistaken identity—deliberately leaving out the part about slipping on the wet floor and ending up in Mike's arms. By the time she got to Brandon's explanation about why the notes she'd sent home with him never reached his uncle, Harriet was laughing so hard she had to wipe away tears.

"So, anyway," Ashley finished up, "Mike is coming in this morning for a conference."

"Oh, so it's 'Mike,' huh?"

"He asked me to call him that. After all, by the time we'd gone through all that. . . ."

"Of course," Harriet said with the utmost seriousness. She opened the door and turned to leave. "I'd better get to my class now. You can fill me in on the rest of the details at lunch. . . ."

Her words trailed off as she almost collided with Mike, who had his hand raised to knock. She took a step backward and surveyed the tall figure in front of her.

"Mr. Shep—Mike, please come in," Ashley invited. As he stepped into the office, it crossed her mind that he looked every bit as attractive in the white shirt and sport coat he was wearing as he had in cutoffs and a tank top. She quickly squelched the thought, however. Summoning a smile, she performed the necessary introductions.

"I'm glad to meet you," Mike said in his deep, rich voice. "I've been learning some rather—interesting things about my nephew." He smiled down at Harriet, revealing even white teeth in a tanned face.

Watching the two people in the doorway shake hands, Ashley noticed that the normally voluble teacher was, for once, at a loss for words. She could have sworn Harriet actually blushed when Mike's hand closed over hers. *He has that effect on women,* she thought dryly. The memory of those few seconds she'd spent in his arms popped into her mind with startling clarity.

Harriet managed to find her voice. "It was nice meeting you, Mr. Shepard." Then, to Ashley, "I have to be going now."

"I'll see you at lunch," Ashley replied.

Harriet's expression indicated that she wouldn't miss it for the world.

"Please have a seat," Ashley said when she was alone with Mike. "I'll get us some coffee before we get started." That would give her a chance to regain her composure. While she busied herself filling two cups from the pot on a small table in the corner, she asked, "Did your new housekeeper ever show up?"

"Yes, she did. She got there shortly after you left."

Ashley handed him a steaming cup. Recalling Sara's comment that "All our housekeepers quit," she asked, "Do you think this one's going to work out?"

"Lord, I hope so," he replied fervently. "She's a middle-aged lady with grandchildren of her own. The kids took to her right away, and she didn't even seem to mind the dog—who, incidentally, is still with us. I'm almost afraid to expect too much, though. Since the kids have been with me, I've had some pretty hair-raising experiences with housekeepers. I wish I could say the situation you walked in on last Saturday was unusual, but the truth is, that was pretty much par for the course around our house. But I won't bore you with my tale of woe. We'd better get started. What's my nephew been up to?''

Ashley hesitated. Now that she'd finally gotten Mike here, she didn't want the conference to deteriorate into simply a recital of Brandon's misdeeds. Still, his uncle had to be aware of what they were up against. ''I—ah—I've been going through Brandon's records.'' She handed a file folder across the desk to him. ''I thought you might want to see for yourself. I've marked the pertinent passages.''

''It goes in the permanent record, huh? When I was a kid, we thought if we did something bad enough that it went into our permanent record, it was going to follow us around the rest of our lives. This won't—''

Although his tone was serious, Ashley caught the twinkle in his eye. ''Don't worry. If he ever runs for public office, I don't think this will turn up on the six o'clock news or on the cover of a supermarket tabloid.''

The banter helped take the edge off a potentially uncomfortable situation, and Mike was smiling as he settled back and opened the folder. His expression gradually turned serious, however, as he studied the sheaf of papers. The lines around his mouth deepened into a frown, and a couple of times his eyebrows shot up.

''A mouse—in a teacher's desk?''

''Actually, it was just a small white mouse—the kind you can get in a pet shop. It was probably even more frightened than Miss Hubbard. Still, she isn't a young woman. The shock—''

''Umm, yes—I see what you mean.'' He closed the

folder and handed it back to her. "So what's the answer? Should I come down hard on Brandon?"

"Here at Soundview we don't like to focus on punishment. We'd rather reinforce good behavior with Student of the Week awards and Good Citizen certificates—that sort of thing."

As she went on to outline some suggestions for modifying Brandon's behavior, Mike couldn't help noticing the way the color of her blouse heightened the blue of her eyes and made her skin look kind of soft and delicate. She should always wear blue, he thought. Blue was definitely her color. . . .

"Don't you agree?" she asked.

"What?"

"I said don't you agree that a system of positive reinforcement would be more effective than punishment?"

"Oh. Of course." Forcing his attention back to the business at hand, he reminded himself he was here to discuss Brandon, not to get all bemused over the color of her eyes.

"He isn't really a bad boy," Ashley continued. "He's just very imaginative. We need to figure out ways to redirect his—ah—creativity. I'll look around and see if I can think of a project he can get involved in that will help him use up some of his energy."

"I'll try whatever you say. I'm new at this parenting business, you know, and I need all the help I can get."

"I see from the children's records that they transferred here from a school in Colorado." Ashley hoped she didn't sound as if she were prying, but she needed to understand the whole situation if she intended to help Brandon. "Had you had much contact with them before they came here?"

"Yes, of course." He sounded surprised that she'd even asked. "My brother and his wife moved to Colorado shortly after they were married, but I made regular trips out there to visit them, especially after their children were born. I wanted my nieces and nephew to have a sense of family."

He paused, and for just a second an expression of pain leaped into his eyes. It was gone so quickly, however, that Ashley wondered if she had imagined it.

"It's a good thing I took the trouble to get to know them," he went on. "When I got word that Dave and Susan had died in a car accident, I flew out there immediately, to make funeral arrangements and to bring the kids back with me. At least they weren't going off with a complete stranger."

"That still must have been very difficult for you and for the children," Ashley murmured sympathetically.

"It was. Jilly cried for days after we got here, poor baby. And she clung to that teddy bear as if it represented the only security in the world. She's adjusted pretty well now, but she hardly lets Woober out of her sight. It took all my powers of persuasion to convince her that bears don't like to go to school."

His expression softened as he spoke of Jillian, and Ashley sensed the little girl occupied a special place in his affections.

"Things were pretty hectic for a while," he went on. "Well, they still are, as you could see from your visit, but it was even worse in the beginning. Fortunately, I had a home to bring them to—people are always talking about what a good investment real estate is, so a few years ago I bought a house. But, of course, I hadn't had the opportunity to make arrangements for a housekeeper before I went to Colorado to get the kids, so when we got back I had no one to look after them.

"I already had a woman who came in a couple of times a week to clean, and I thought it would be a simple matter to ask her to work for me full-time, but she made it clear right away that she doesn't 'do children.' So while the kids were still trying to adjust to everything that had happened, I was frantically trying to find a suitable housekeeper. It wasn't a matter of money—I make a more than adequate salary. But there are some things money can't buy."

Ashley felt a stab of sympathy as he went on to recount some of his experiences with household help.

"And all this time there were things going on at the plant that needed my attention," he continued. "We're working on a new design, and it still has a lot of bugs in it. Even though the kids needed me, I couldn't just turn my back on my responsibilities at work—we have deadlines to meet and contracts to fulfill. I've been trying to do the best I can for everyone, but—well, sometimes I feel that I'm treading water frantically and if I stop for a moment I'll sink."

Ashley's heart went out to him. She was beginning to understand how mistaken she'd been in her assessment of him as uncaring or disinterested in the children's welfare. He was just an ordinary guy who had been caught up in circumstances beyond his control, and he was trying to make the best of things.

When Mike caught Ashley's expression of sympathy, he realized he'd revealed more of his situation than he'd intended to. What was he doing, telling all this stuff to someone he barely knew? He didn't want her to get the idea he couldn't look after his own family.

But after what he'd told her, Ashley felt obligated to offer some sort of suggestion. She realized she'd have to tread carefully. She wouldn't want to overstep her bounds. "Mike," she began thoughtfully, "have you ever considered that you might have taken on more than you can handle by accepting the responsibility of raising three children? Have you thought about asking for some kind of outside help—"

The mention of "outside help" triggered a warning signal in Mike's brain. He'd thought Ashley was genuinely concerned about his children, but it appeared she was just like all the rest. Counselors, social workers—they were all alike, only interested in taking over. The next thing he knew, some know-it-all bureaucratic type would be swooping down and whisking his kids away to someplace where they would be "properly cared for."

His explosive "No!" took Ashley by surprise. He stood up, as if to indicate the conference was over. "Thank you for your ideas on improving Brandon's behavior," he said stiffly. "As for the rest of what we discussed, forget I said anything. My kids and I will manage just fine without anyone else's help." With that, he turned and walked out, leaving Ashley staring after him.

That was a close call, Mike thought as he strode out of the building. He was remembering the way he and his brother had been hustled off to a foster home by social workers when his mother had been too ill to care for them properly.

He realized now, of course, that it had been necessary. With their mother too sick to earn a living or look after them—their dad had walked out on the family years earlier—foster care was the only answer. But at five years of age, all he could see was that he and Davey were being torn from their mother and all that was dear and familiar to them and being sent off to live with strangers. Davey—all of ten years old at the time—had done his best to comfort him, but Mike could still recall how he'd cried himself to sleep night after night.

His mother's condition had deteriorated quickly, and she'd died the following year, leaving her two sons to be raised in a succession of foster homes and institutions. Granted, not all of the places had been too bad. There were a lot of foster parents who were truly caring people. Still, there had always been the awareness that he didn't really belong to them, that he was only there temporarily. And the very worst times had been when he and Davey had to be separated because there were no homes available that had room for two children.

No, the last thing he needed was other people interfering in his life. He and his little family would manage just fine on their own. He wasn't going to allow outsiders to mess up his kids' lives the way they had his and Davey's.

Besides, he'd always prided himself on being able

to stand on his own two feet, without depending on anyone else. True, there was that time, back when he was just starting out, that he'd had to accept help, but that had been strictly a business deal. And he'd paid back everything he'd received.

His thoughts went back twelve years, to when he was just finishing his second year of college. He'd used up all the scholarships and student loans that had been available, and he had despaired of acquiring even a basic college degree, let alone the advanced training he'd need in order to fulfill his dream of becoming an aerospace engineer.

Then, out of the blue, he'd been approached by a delegation from Flint Aircraft, who were scouting the college in much the same way as recruiters for pro-football teams, in search of the brightest and most promising students. The offer they'd made him was simple: The company would finance his education, as well as seeing that he received the necessary on-the-job training, in return for his promise to come work for them for an agreed-on period of time. It had seemed too good to refuse, and he'd agreed without hesitation.

He'd realized, of course, that they considered him an investment, and he'd resolved to do everything in his power to make sure they got their money's worth. Although they were willing to back him, he knew it was up to him to keep his part of the bargain.

Now, twelve years later, he'd more than fulfilled his obligation to the company, and he was free to seek employment elsewhere. He was perfectly content at Flint, however, and had no desire to change jobs. He was doing exactly what he'd always wanted to do, and his employers had made it clear, through the promotions and raises that came his way regularly, that their faith in him had been justified.

No, even though he'd gotten a lucky break, he'd achieved his present success through hard work and determination. He'd never been in the habit of accepting help from others, and he didn't intend to start now.

The way the conference had ended put a damper on the rest of Ashley's morning. As she went about her duties, the image of Mike's eyes suddenly turning cold and his mouth setting in a firm, unyielding line kept intruding into her thoughts.

What had she said to set him off? she wondered. She'd only meant to suggest that he might want to enlist the help of some other relatives. Surely the children must have grandparents or other aunts and uncles. But this was obviously a touchy subject with him.

Harriet was waiting for her when she entered the teachers' lounge at lunchtime. "You didn't tell me your Mr. Shepard was a hunk of the first order," she said accusingly.

Ashley felt the sudden flush of heat that spread over her cheeks. Why did people—first Stewart and then Harriet—keep referring to Mike as *her* Mr. Shepard? "He doesn't *belong* to me," she pointed out.

"Just the same, you never mentioned the guy was drop-dead gorgeous," Harriet went on.

Ashley was relieved when several other teachers came into the lounge just then. At least now she'd be spared having to discuss Mike Shepard's physical attributes.

But apparently it wasn't to be. "You must have had a really interesting morning," one of the newcomers commented, addressing her remarks to Ashley. "I was on my way to class this morning when this absolutely *fabulous*-looking guy asked me how to get to your office."

"Oh, that was the uncle of one of the students," Ashley explained. "We had an appointment for a conference this morning."

But she knew she was in for some good-natured teasing, as all heads turned toward her and several sets of eyebrows rose. Was this some kind of conspiracy? she wondered irritably. Was Mike Shepard everybody's favorite topic of conversation today? So he was good-looking. Big deal. Judging from the way this morning's conference had ended, he obviously had a few things to learn about common courtesy.

Chapter Five

It had been several days since Mike's conference with that counselor at the kids' school, and he was still smarting over her implication that he needed outside help to raise his brother's children.

Maybe it had been his own fault, he thought as he tossed his shaving kit into the open overnight bag on his bed. But she'd seemed so interested, and having someone to talk to had been a pleasant change. He'd started feeling kind of relaxed, and the next thing he knew, he was telling her a lot of stuff he should have kept to himself. True, there'd been a few problems—there were bound to be when you suddenly found yourself with a ready-made family—but nothing he couldn't handle.

His thoughts were interrupted by a light tap on his bedroom door. In answer to his "Come in," Mrs. Jackson bustled into the room, carrying some neatly folded shirts.

"I ironed these as soon as you said you were going out of town," she said. "I thought you might need them."

"Thanks." He accepted the garments she held out

to him. "I really appreciate your agreeing to stay with the kids tonight without any advance notice."

"It's no problem at all. Before the children get in from school, I'll just run home and pick up a few things I'll need if I'm going to be here overnight, and then I'll be all set."

"If you're going out, it might be a good idea to do it this morning," he advised, glancing out the window at the bank of dark clouds forming. "It looks like we're in for quite a storm later today."

"Oh, I intend to be back before it breaks," the housekeeper replied. "I never did like driving in the rain."

Thank goodness for Mrs. Jackson, he thought when she'd gone out. Things were running much more smoothly since he'd hired her. With a cheerful, down-to-earth practicality, she was quickly whipping his household into shape. She even had Dawg—who, it seemed, was becoming a member of the family—under her spell. Somehow she'd gotten the idea across to the big, somewhat hyperactive animal that if he hoped to stick around, he'd better clean up his act. A word from her, and he almost tripped over his own feet in an effort to please her.

Mike wished he could persuade her to "live in," but she had her own little house in a rural area just outside town and had no desire to give up her privacy and independence. She arrived bright and early every weekday morning to fix breakfast and get the kids off to school, though, and was on hand when they came home, to dispense snacks, oversee homework, and maintain order. And she'd promised to be available for evening sitting, or to stay the night when he had to go out of town on an occasional business trip—such as this one to southern California, which had come up so suddenly.

The problem had developed this morning during a routine test. It had finally been traced to a control module that was being manufactured by MagnaTech, a subsidiary of Flint Aircraft. Although the glitch was relatively minor and they could work around it for a time, eventually production schedules would be delayed until it was ironed out. A hurried conference had been held, the result of which was that Mike would go down and meet with the engineers at MagnaTech in person.

"I hate to ask you to go on such short notice," the chief engineer, Tom Fenton, had apologized. Tom was aware of Mike's home situation and wasn't unsympathetic to his problems as a single parent. "I don't see what else we can do, though. This project has been your baby right from the start, and if we send anyone else, it'll just result in more delays."

"Sure, I understand," Mike had said. "Just give me time to get packed and to square it with my housekeeper."

Mrs. Jackson had promised to hold the fort for him here at home, and at this moment one of the company planes was standing by to fly him to Los Angeles. Not that he wanted to go—in spite of the attendant problems, he enjoyed his new family and had no desire to be a long-distance parent. Besides, he hadn't even had a chance to explain to the kids why he had to go away.

He consoled himself with the thought that if all went

well, he and the MagnaTech people would have the problem settled by this evening, and he would be back home tomorrow morning, almost before anyone even had time to miss him. He finished his packing, checked to make sure he had everything he needed, and closed the bag.

"Don't worry about a thing," Mrs. Jackson reassured him when he went into the kitchen to leave a number where he could be reached. "I know you don't like leaving without having a chance to say good-bye to the children, but I'll have a talk with them. I'll make sure they understand it couldn't be helped."

Ashley listened to the ringing of the telephone without making any move to get up and answer it. She knew it was Stewart. He'd been trying to call her all week.

She'd found a message from him on her answering machine Monday evening when she'd returned from a faculty meeting. "Give me a call as soon as you get in," he'd said. Although the words themselves were innocuous, there was a peremptory undertone to his voice that had sent a surge of irritation through her. Who did he think he was? she thought resentfully—*ordering* her to call him?

Even if she'd wanted to talk to him, she wouldn't have been able to return the call right then, anyway. She had to go over the notes from the meeting, write up a list of the recommendations that had been discussed, and make preparations for a conference she had coming up first thing in the morning.

The next time she spoke to Stewart, she wanted it

to be when she told him she didn't care to see him again, and that wasn't something she could rush through. She had no doubt he'd try to brush aside her arguments. She needed time to decide just what to say to make him understand she meant business. She filed "call Stewart" under her mental list of unpleasant chores that had to be dealt with.

He'd tried to contact her several more times, sounding more and more annoyed with each message he left on her machine. She wasn't in the habit of procrastinating, but she found herself inventing excuses for not getting back to him. Although she knew it was cowardly of her, she continued letting the machine screen her calls. She eased her conscience by reminding herself that it had been a busy week, with several matters vying for her attention, and she simply couldn't spare the time right now for a confrontation with Stewart.

Now Bridget jumped lightly up onto the arm of the chair next to the telephone. She glanced from her mistress to the jangling instrument and back to Ashley again.

"I don't *have* to answer it," Ashley said defensively in response to Bridget's *meow?* "It *is* my telephone."

After the fourth ring the answering machine took over, with a brief, impersonal message stating that she couldn't come to the phone right now and asking the caller to leave a name and number.

There was a short pause, and then a soft, timid voice—little more than a whisper—asked, "Miss Kendall, are you there?"

Surprised, Ashley picked up the phone. "Sara? Is that you?"

"Yes, this is Sara. Miss Kendall, I—I don't know what to do, and you were the only person I could think of to call." It was obvious, from the catch in her voice, that something was wrong.

Ashley's experience with children told her it could be anything from being in actual physical danger to not having the right dress to wear to a classmate's party. And even that, she knew, could take on monumental proportions. She willed a calmness into her voice before asking, "What seems to be the problem?"

"I'm trying to take care of Jilly and Brandon, but Jilly's crying because she's scared of the thunder and lightning, and Brandon won't behave. . . ." Her words trailed off on a note of panic.

"Wait a minute, honey, I'm afraid you've lost me. Back up just a little. Why are *you* taking care of Jilly and Brandon? Where is your uncle?"

"I don't know. He—he hasn't come home yet."

Ashley felt a surge of anger toward Mike. Where *was* he, anyway? Out on a date? She had a brief vision of the red sports car pulling up in front of one of Tacoma's livelier night spots, with a glamorous blonde in the passenger seat. Surely the man must realize how unsettling his absence could be to a child who had just recently lost both of her parents.

She reminded herself that he had a right to a social life. But he also had a responsibility to his children to make sure the housekeeper he'd hired to look after them was sympathetic to their needs. If this Mrs. Jackson was the "jewel" he seemed to think she was, why wasn't she giving Sara the comfort and reassurance she needed right now?

For that matter, why wasn't she doing a better job of looking after the children? Sara shouldn't have to call an outsider to tell her that her brother was misbehaving and her sister was afraid of the storm.

"Mrs. Jackson *is* taking care of you, isn't she?"

"She—she's *supposed* to be," Sara replied in a small voice.

Well, then, why wasn't she doing it? Ashley wondered hotly. An image popped into her mind of a frumpy, disinterested woman sprawled in front of the television set, leaving the children to fend for themselves.

Maybe Ashley was overstepping her bounds, but if the housekeeper was neglecting her duties, somebody needed to speak to her about it, for the children's sake. "Sara, would you have Mrs. Jackson come to the phone?" she said.

There was a brief pause, then, "She isn't here, either. She's always here when we get home from school, and she stays until Uncle Mike comes, b-but she wasn't here today."

This was absolutely unbelievable. This woman had made a commitment to look after the children. Didn't she have any sense of responsibility at all? "You mean *nobody* is there with you?" Ashley asked.

"Just Jilly and Brandon, and—and I can't take care of them. . . ."

Ashley winced as a flash of thunder illuminated the sky outside her window, followed closely by the low, menacing rumble of thunder. Sara's words were drowned out by the crackle of static on the line.

"Miss Kendall—are you still there?"

"Yes, I'm here." Ashley forced a light note into her tone. "I'm sure your uncle will be home before long, but why don't I come over and stay with you until he gets there?"

"You're coming over?" Her relief was evident. "Oh, *please* get here as soon as you can."

"I'll leave right away. And, Sara?"

"Yes, Miss Kendall?"

"You tell Brandon to behave himself, or he'll have to answer to me."

"Sure, I'll tell him that," Sara replied with what was a brave attempt at a giggle, but ended up as more of a sob.

Taking time only to slip into her raincoat and gather her purse and keys, Ashley was soon on her way. As she drove to the Shepard house, she hardly noticed the rain coming down in sheets and the way the wind was whipping the tree branches. Her mind was awhirl with all the things she intended to say to Mike when she saw him. As she pulled up in front of the house, she took several deep, calming breaths before getting out of the car so her anger wouldn't communicate itself to the children. That would only make the situation worse.

Before she could ring the bell, the front door flew open. "I'm so glad you're here," Sara burst out, grabbing her hand and pulling her inside. Her voice was shaky, and it was clear, from the telltale gleam in her eyes, that tears were very close to the surface. Jilly, clutching Woober, came up on Ashley's other side and slipped a hand into her free one trustingly. Even Dawg came rushing out to greet her, grinning a big, doggy grin, his bushy tail wagging. Only Brandon, standing in the background, didn't seem altogether happy to see her.

The reason was obvious, when the girls escorted her into the house. Their brother had obviously been making the most of an evening with no authority figure present. The living room had a cluttered appearance, due mostly to Brandon's belongings strewn about. His jacket was draped across the arm of a chair, comic books littered the floor, and beneath the coffee table lay several video-game cartridges. A couple of overturned sofa cushions completed the impression of utter confusion.

Well, first things first, Ashley decided. Taking stock of the situation, she said, "I don't suppose you've had any dinner, have you?"

"I heated up some soup and made sandwiches," Sara replied. "And we had apples."

Well, it may not have been haute cuisine, but it sounded like a fairly balanced meal, Ashley thought. At least they hadn't gone hungry.

"We were going to load the dishwasher and clean up the kitchen," Sara went on, "but Brandon wouldn't help."

Ashley assessed her position. Although she hadn't asked for the job, it seemed that she was in charge of these children for the time being. The girls would be no problem, of course, but Brandon was another matter. She sensed that if she didn't seize the upper hand immediately, she was in for a rough evening. On the other hand, she didn't want to take a chance on alienating him.

"You haven't had any dessert, have you?" she asked.

"We wanted to have some cookies, but we're not supposed to get into the cookie jar without asking, and there wasn't anybody to ask," Jilly explained virtuously.

"What would you say to popcorn and fudge? I'm probably the world's number-one fudge maker, you know."

This suggestion met with instant approval from all three children. They clustered around her with offers to help.

With the promise of fudge and popcorn once the living room and kitchen were put to rights, Ashley soon had her young charges bustling around getting things in order. All right, she knew it was out-and-out bribery, and it went against all her training—not to mention what the fudge would likely do to their teeth. She eased her conscience by reminding herself that drastic situations called for drastic measures.

Before long the kitchen was a scene of pleasant confusion as Ashley stirred the pan of fudge bubbling on the stove, while the children tended the popcorn. Dawg sat in the middle of the floor, getting in everyone's way and sniffing appreciatively.

The storm outside was forgotten as they all gathered in the den to munch fudge and popcorn and play video games. Dawg watched their every move, ready to pounce any time a morsel fell on the floor. Every so often he put a shaggy paw on the sofa and looked up at them with large, soulful eyes, as if to remind them that he was hungry too.

"Hot dog!" Brandon cried as he shot down another Zarquoid supply ship. "Now I can use my Sidewinder Missiles."

"Don't get too confident. I still have one more Energy Capsule," Ashley reminded him.

"Don't forget, I get to play the winner," Sara put in. She had already shown a surprisingly competitive streak by beating both both her brother and Ashley.

Jilly snuggled close to Ashley and smiled up at her. "We're having fun, aren't we, Ashley?" In order to foster a feeling of closeness between herself and the children, Ashley had suggested they call her by her first name rather than the more formal Miss Kendall they used at school.

"Yes, we are," Ashley replied, giving her a hug.

"I know what!" Jilly exclaimed, her dark eyes shining. "Why don't you come here and live with us, and you and Uncle Mike can be our mommy and daddy."

Sara gave her a look of big-sisterly superiority. "Don't be silly. They'd have to be married to be our mom and dad."

"Oh." Jilly considered this, then brightened. She held her hands palm up, in a gesture that indicated the solution was obvious. "You and Uncle Mike could *get* married."

At that moment Brandon dropped some popcorn as he raised a handful to his mouth. Dawg, nuzzling around the floor like a vacuum cleaner, lunged for it with such vigor that he almost overturned the coffee table. In the scramble to keep everything on it from spilling, Ashley was spared the necessity of a reply to Jilly's remark.

"Isn't it about time you kids went to bed?" Ashley asked a little while later, when she noticed Jilly yawning.

"Just a couple more games," they all begged, reminding her that tomorrow was Saturday.

Outnumbered, she gave in. Half an hour later, though, Jilly was almost asleep with her head in Ashley's lap, Sara's eyelids were drooping, and Brandon's normal high spirits seemed to have deserted him. This time even Brandon offered only a token protest.

As the two older children went ahead with their own preparations, Ashley helped Jilly with her usual night-time ritual, which included elaborate good nights to all of her stuffed animals. "And a drink of orange juice," Jilly said when she was at last tucked into bed, with Woober beside her.

Ashley started to reply, *Not after you've brushed your teeth,* but instead she gave a little shrug. So many of the rules had already been broken, what did one more matter? "Coming right up." She started down the hall to the kitchen.

"In the Strawberry Shortcake mug," Jilly called after her, milking the situation for all it was worth.

As Ashley withdrew the large pitcher of juice from the refrigerator, Dawg spotted a stray popcorn kernel on the kitchen floor. Making a dash for it, he bumped against Ashley, almost knocking her down. While she was struggling to maintain her balance, almost half the contents of the pitcher sloshed over the rim and down the front of her sweatshirt and jeans. She gave an exclamation of dismay as the cold, sticky liquid soaked through her clothes and made contact with her skin.

A pajama-clad Sara appeared in the doorway. "I'm going to bed now. I just came out to say good night. . . ." Her voice trailed off as she spotted the large stain on Ashley's clothes. "Oh, yuck!"

"That's right—oh, yuck," Ashley agreed, pulling her wet shirt away from her body. She couldn't go around like this. It felt awful. "Sara honey, is there anything around here I could put on for a little while, so I can rinse out my clothes?"

"Sure. I'll go see what I can find."

While Ashley waited for Sara's return, she wiped up the spilled juice from the kitchen floor, then poured more juice into a Strawberry Shortcake mug and took it in to Jilly. The little girl drew the bedtime ritual out as long as possible, but finally Ashley gave her a hug and a kiss and, with a whispered good night, turned off her light.

As Ashley tiptoed out of Jilly's room, Sara appeared in the hallway with a deep-blue velour garment. "Here's Uncle Mike's bathrobe. I know it'll be miles too big, but it was all I could find."

Ashley was somewhat taken aback. It hadn't occurred to her that the only clothes available would be Mike's. It seemed so—so *personal* to be wearing something of his. Especially a bathrobe. *Don't be silly,* she told herself briskly. She had to have something to put on until her own things were fit to be worn again.

In the bathroom she changed into the robe, which was so roomy she had to wrap it almost twice around herself before knotting the belt securely. Even then she had to keep pulling the top up, as it had a tendency to slip down over one shoulder. A whiff of Mike's after-shave that clung to the garment wafted toward her, evoking a brief, provocative recollection of those few seconds she'd spent in his strong, warm embrace. She rinsed the juice from her shirt and jeans under the faucet, scrubbing vigorously, as if she could wash away the memory.

When she emerged from the bathroom, she tossed her things into the dryer in the utility room just off the kitchen and turned the setting up on High. She fervently hoped Mike wouldn't show up until she was dressed in her own clothes again. She felt she'd be under a distinct disadvantage if she had to confront him wearing *his* bathrobe.

While she waited for her jeans and shirt to dry, she wandered through the house, turning off most of the lights, closing drapes, and making sure doors were locked. As she switched off the living-room lamps, she eyed the sofa. It looked awfully inviting, with that thick comforter tossed over the back of it.

Even though she'd enjoyed spending the evening with the children, the awareness had been there, in the back of her mind, that the reason she was here was because they had been virtually abandoned by their uncle. Her determination to keep them from realizing this, along with her anger at Mike, had taken a toll on her, both emotionally and physically. Now that the children were in bed and she could let her guard down, she realized she felt incredibly weary.

She sank down on the sofa and pulled the comforter over her. Soon she would get up and take her clothes out of the dryer and get dressed, but just for a little while she wanted to lie here and unwind. . . .

* * *

It was a relief to be back. Mike's trip to California had been productive, but he was glad it was over. He and the engineers at MagnaTech had worked far into the night, examining the problem from every angle. It was past midnight when they'd finally pinpointed the source of the trouble. After several minor adjustments, the last few tests they'd run had gone smoothly. Confident that the glitch had been ironed out, he'd gone back to his hotel to fall into bed and catch a few hours' sleep. It would have suited him just fine to start home right away. He'd forced himself to wait until morning, however, out of consideration for his pilot, who was probably right in the middle of a sound sleep.

Driving home, Mike could tell that yesterday's storm had been a real gully-washer. Even in the early-morning half light, he could see the twigs and branches that littered the ground, and several times he had to swerve around deep puddles in the road.

As he pulled into his driveway, some slight inconsistency nagged at the edges of his awareness. What was it that seemed somehow out of sync?

The car parked in front of his house. That was it. It didn't seem to be the one he remembered seeing Mrs. Jackson drive. But with his attention focused on the modifications that had to be made to the control module, and the report he would make to Tom Fenton, he gave it little thought. He had other matters on his mind.

He let himself into the house quietly and set his belongings down just inside the door so he could fend off Dawg's enthusiastic greeting. Nobody else seemed to be up and about yet. The lights were still off, and the drapes hadn't been opened.

Making his way through the semidark living room, he spotted the blanket-covered form on the sofa. That was odd, he thought. Why was Mrs. Jackson sleeping out here when there was a perfectly comfortable guest room at her disposal?

As he tiptoed past, being careful not to waken her, a puzzled frown creased his forehead. He'd always thought of his housekeeper as—well, not exactly stout, but at least sturdy. The figure on the sofa was so slight he might not have even noticed anyone was there—he would have simply thought the comforter had been left carelessly bunched up—if it hadn't been for the even, regular breathing. Well, maybe one of the kids had wandered out here and fallen asleep.

Curious, he leaned over for a closer look, then stepped back as the figure stirred slightly.

With a soft little sigh Ashley snuggled deeper under the comforter and buried her face in the collar of the velour robe. The brief movement released the aroma of Mike's after-shave—fresh, tangy, and overpoweringly *male*.

Unexpectedly, as she hovered in that elusive dreamlike state between sleep and wakefulness, a tangled swirl of half-remembered sensations intruded into the shadowy haze of her subconscious. Her mind and emotions replayed those few moments in the hallway when a second or two of inattention had thrown her into Mike's embrace. Her fingers could feel the warmth of his body, where her hands had flattened against his chest. She heard his heartbeat beneath her ear as his arms had tightened around her to keep her from falling. Or was that her own heart thudding so wildly?

Her entire body tingled with sudden awareness as the flood of memories came rushing back with startling vividness.

"Mike." Involuntarily she whispered his name.

"Ashley?" His deep voice, like gentle fingers massaging her spine, penetrated through the swirling cobwebs.

When had the dream ended and reality taken over? she wondered, fighting her way back to a conscious state. Or was she still dreaming? As her sleep-fogged brain struggled to reason this out, she pushed away whatever was covering her face—something soft and downy—and found herself looking directly into the compelling depths of Mike's dark eyes!

This has *to be a dream,* she told herself, confused. Otherwise why would he be here in front of her, so near that his presence evoked a soft quiver inside her?

So near she could almost feel his mouth, warm and gentle, on hers.

So near that her own lips parted with anticipation.

Chapter Six

"Uncle Mike, you're home!"

Jilly's voice cut through Ashley's dreamlike state and jerked her sharply back to reality. It was morning, and she'd spent the night on Mike's sofa, while he'd— Just where had *he* been all night?

She thrust the comforter aside and stood up, intending to tell Mike exactly what she thought of a man who would leave three children unattended overnight— which they would have been if she hadn't come over to look after them. Obviously he was just now getting in.

Too late, she remembered what she was wearing. Before she could deliver the angry tirade that was building up inside her, the robe started to slip down over one shoulder. She made a grab for it and caught it in time to preserve her modesty.

Mike stared at Ashley in utter bewilderment. Before he could say anything, Jilly ran to him and threw herself into his arms. While his attention was thus diverted, Ashley retied her belt and made other adjustments to her attire.

In spite of the disapproval radiating from her, it

crossed Mike's mind that she looked cute as the dickens in that oversized bathrobe, with her hair all sleep-tousled— But what the heck was she doing here—and in his robe?

"Oh, I forgot Woober." Jilly unwound her arms from around Mike and went to retrieve her beloved bear.

"It's about time you decided to come home," Ashley said in a voice thick with sarcasm when Jilly had left the room. From her expression it was obvious she would consider drawing and quartering none too good for him. "What kind of man are you, anyway, going off and leaving these children by themselves?"

Quite clearly, this wasn't a rhetorical question. Mike took a step or two backward, stunned by the force of her vehemence. Before he could formulate any sensible answer, Jilly returned, clutching Woober.

"You didn't come home yesterday," the little girl said in an accusing tone. "Where *were* you?"

"I—I had to go on a trip. Didn't Mrs. Jackson explain that?"

"No. She wasn't here when we got home from school. *Nobody* was here. We got scared—just a *little*, because of the thunder and lightning, you know—so Sara called Ashley, and she came over and stayed with us. We had lots of fun after she got here. She made popcorn and fudge, and we played video games—" Jilly chattered away, oblivious to the hostile looks Ashley was darting at her uncle and to his own bewildered expression.

"Mrs. Jackson—she was supposed to stay with the kids. . . ." Mike's words trailed off. Already thrown off balance at finding Ashley there instead of Mrs. Jackson, he was having difficulty organizing his thoughts. He tried again. "I had to go down to Los Angeles. We were having trouble with a control module— Well, the reason I went isn't important. Anyway, the trip came up unexpectedly yesterday morning. Mrs. Jackson was here when I left, and she agreed to stay overnight—and to explain to the kids."

Ashley folded her arms and glared at him. "Well, then, what happened to her?"

Mike shook his head, still puzzled by this unusual turn of events. "I can't believe she'd let the kids down this way. She seemed so dependable—"

He broke off and strode to the telephone with the air of a man determined to get to the bottom of things. When he punched Mrs. Jackson's number, a series of beeps and squawks came over the line, followed by a recorded message informing him that number was not in service. Ashley looked at him with a skeptical expression as he hung up.

While Mike frowned at the telephone, trying to decide what to do next, it rang, almost as if he had willed it to do so.

"Oh, Mr. Shepard," Mrs. Jackson's voice came over the line. She sounded distraught. "The children— are they all right?"

"Yes, they're fine," he replied coldly. *No thanks to you,* he was tempted to add, but he restrained himself.

"I'm so sorry. If there was anything I could have done—" She seemed on the verge of tears. "It was the storm. You remember I told you I'd have to go home and get a few things so I could spend the night with the children? Well, the storm was at its height just as I was ready to start back. I was just about to get into my car when a limb from this big fir tree in my yard came crashing down on top of my car. It caved the roof right in. I went back in the house and tried to call someone to take me into town, but the limb also knocked out the telephone line. I'm calling from my daughter's house now. When she couldn't get me on the phone this morning, she came over to check on me.''

"Are you all right?'' Mike asked, concerned. Mrs. Jackson wasn't a young woman, and he realized what a frightening experience it must have been for her to watch her car being demolished by a tree—especially just seconds before she would have been in it.

"Yes, I'm fine, except for being a bit shaken,'' the housekeeper replied. "I was going to ask my neighbor to drive me in,'' she explained, "but he wasn't home. My next nearest neighbor is over a mile away. I tried to get there, but the rain was coming down so hard, and the wind was blowing—it was all I could do just to stand up. I finally had to go back.''

A mental image of the good-hearted woman attempting to fight her way through a storm to fulfill her commitment to his children made Mike immediately contrite for any doubts he'd had about her loyalty.

"I've been just frantic, worrying about the children being there alone,'' Mrs. Jackson went on. "I promised you I'd be there to look after them, and I let you down—'' Her voice broke.

"Now, Mrs. Jackson, it wasn't your fault,'' Mike

hastened to reassure her. "It was just one of those things nobody could have predicted. And the children weren't alone. Sara called—ah—a family friend who came over and stayed with them. They were fine."

When Mike finished his phone conversation, he turned back to Ashley. "My faith in human nature has been restored. I knew Mrs. Jackson wouldn't just abandon the kids." Briefly he explained the circumstances that had prevented the housekeeper from getting there.

Ashley's expression immediately changed from suspicious to sympathetic. "The poor woman. What a terrible thing to happen!"

"I got the impression she was more concerned about not being able to get to the kids than she was over her own danger. I can't tell you how grateful I am that you stepped in to take over."

"I didn't do anything special," Ashley replied modestly. She gave a little shrug, and the slight movement sent the robe sliding again, exposing one shoulder. With as much aplomb as she could muster, she pulled it back up.

Mike managed to keep his expression deadpan, except for the twinkle in his eye. "I must say, you certainly look better in that robe than I ever did," he couldn't resist saying.

A splash of color stained Ashley's cheeks as she pulled the garment closer around her. "I suppose I'd better get dressed."

"Um—yes, that might be a good idea. Before you go, though, do you mind if I ask just *why* you're dressed that way?"

"Oh. I was pouring some juice for Jilly, and that—that animal ran into me."

Mike nodded, as if he understood perfectly. "He does get a little rambunctious. Did he hurt you?"

"Only my dignity." It was difficult to stand there and make conversation with a man (especially one as attractive as Mike, a little voice inside her said) while clad in a bathrobe—his robe—that was in danger of falling right off her.

At that moment Sara appeared in the doorway in rumpled pajamas, with a sleepy Brandon close behind. At the sight of Mike, Brandon rushed into the room and flung himself at his uncle. Sara followed with a little more decorum.

Ashley took advantage of the diversion to slip away. She retrieved her clothes from the dryer and headed toward the bathroom, while the children chattered excitedly to Mike about their adventures of the evening before.

When she emerged a short while later, dressed in her own clothes, she felt more in control of the situation. Following the aroma of freshly brewed coffee, she found Mike in the kitchen. "Where are the children?" she asked.

"They're in the den, watching cartoons," Mike said, handing her a cup of coffee. "I shudder to think of what could have happened if they'd been here alone all night. Oh, the girls would probably have managed all right—Sara can look after herself and Jilly too. But the way Brandon's mind works, he could have set the house on fire conducting 'experiments,' or tried to parachute off the roof with an umbrella. I know I've already said it, but I have to tell you again how much I appreciate your coming to their rescue.''

"It was nothing," Ashley protested. "Anyone would have done the same."

"No, I don't think 'anyone' would have. To tell you the truth, I can't think of a single other person I know who would have dropped everything to come over and stay with them.''

Ashley thought this over as she took a sip of the hot, bracing coffee. She recalled the interview in her office that had ended on such a disastrous note when she'd tried to suggest that he might consider seeking help from family members. She realized she could be treading on thin ice, but she felt duty bound to bring the matter up again. If he had some kind of macho male pride that made him think he had to carry the entire burden alone, it was time he swallowed that pride.

A heavy knot formed in the pit of her stomach at the thought of confronting him on what was obviously a touchy subject with him. She wrapped her hands around the coffee mug to keep them from trembling. "You know, Mike, raising three children is a big responsibility. It wouldn't hurt to accept some help now and then.''

His eyes narrowed, and his features hardened into an impassive expression. "We've already discussed this. I thought I made it clear that I'm not going to have social workers interfering in my family, taking the kids off to be cared for by strangers and shunting them from one foster home to another.''

Ashley's jaw dropped in surprise. "Social workers? Is that what you thought I meant?"

"Well, didn't you?"

"No, of course not. What I had in mind was allowing other relatives to help out—grandparents, aunts, and uncles. . . ." Her words trailed off as she caught the way his mouth twisted into a grim line. *Now* what had she said? she wondered. Maybe there was some sort of family feud going on.

"There isn't anyone else," Mike said. "Dave was my only relative. Our mother died when I was six. And Susan had no family, either."

"Oh." Ashley's monosyllable came out sounding small and flat. She couldn't imagine what it must be like to have no one to call your own, no one to turn to if you needed a shoulder to cry on, someone to share a triumph, or just a listening ear. She herself came from a large, noisy, friendly clan. Although most of her relatives lived over near Wenatchee, in the apple-growing area of the state, and she didn't get to see them as often as she'd have liked, she knew they were available if she needed them.

"I should never have brought it up," she said, genuinely contrite. "It's none of my business."

"That's all right. You had no way of knowing, and you were only trying to be helpful. Look, I'm sorry about the way I reacted when you brought it up that day in your office, but I'm afraid I misunderstood what you were getting at."

He hesitated slightly before going on. "When Dave and I were small and our mother got sick, we were unceremoniously whisked off and put in foster homes.

I realize now, of course, that it was necessary, but at the time all I could see was that we were being separated from our mother and from each other. And the way it was done left a lasting impression. Nobody seemed to understand or care that we were just two frightened little boys.'' He rubbed a hand across his eyes, as if to wipe away the memory. ''When Dave and Susan were killed in that auto accident,'' he continued, ''I made up my mind I'd never let that happen to their children.''

Ashley could tell, from the shadow that fell across his face, how painful the subject was to him. ''I really am sorry. I was butting in where I had no right—''

''No, you had the kids' best interests at heart. I had no right to get on my high horse that way. Truce?'' He extended his hand in a conciliatory gesture and smiled so engagingly that any vestige of resentment Ashley might have had vanished like a wisp of smoke.

''Truce,'' she agreed. As his hand closed over hers, a warm, tingly sensation traveled through her fingers and up her arm. All at once awareness came out of nowhere and leaped between them. Ashley found herself gazing at his lips and wondering how they would feel on hers. . . .

''Hey, when are we gonna eat? I'm hungry.'' Brandon's voice brought her back to reality. All three children were standing in the doorway.

''I—I have to be going,'' Ashley said.

Mike looked disappointed. ''Can't you stay and have breakfast with us? I was going to make waffles.''

''I really need to get home. I have to—to—'' She couldn't think of any valid reason why she had to leave right away. She just knew she needed to put some space between herself and Mike—she was shaken by the effect his closeness had on her. She realized her hand was still in his, and she withdrew it as unobtrusively as she could.

Cheeks flaming, she gathered up her belongings. "Thanks again for your help," Mike called after her as she made a hasty exit.

As Ashley let herself into her apartment, she saw there were several messages on her answering machine. She played them back while she refilled Bridget's food and water dishes. They were all from Stewart, and they sounded increasingly irritated. "Ashley, we have to talk," the last one said. "I'll be over this afternoon."

"Looks like this is it," she said to Bridget with a resigned shrug. Sooner or later she was going to have to face Stewart, so she might as well get it over with.

There's really no reason to make such a big deal out of this, she told herself. *I'll just make it clear to him that there's absolutely nothing between us. He'll have to accept that.*

In spite of having given herself this little pep talk, she couldn't suppress a flicker of anxiety when she saw a shiny new BMW pulling into the parking lot. When Stewart got out, she could tell by the way he marched up to the building entrance that this wasn't going to be easy. Even the ringing of the doorbell had a peremptory tone to it.

She arranged her features into what she hoped was just the right touch of courtesy, blended with a steadfast resolve, before answering the door. *Polite but firm,* she reminded herself. She had no intention of being drawn into a verbal skirmish.

"Stewart, please come—"

He strode into her apartment before she could finish the sentence. Ashley noticed that Bridget came over immediately to wind around his ankles. He glanced down, a slight frown creasing his forehead. Why was it, she wondered, that cats always seemed to sense when someone didn't like cats and made a beeline for that person?

"Why haven't you returned any of my calls?" he demanded without preamble.

Her nervousness gave way to a flash of irritation. Who did he think he was? "I've been busy," she said, raising her chin a fraction of an inch. "I do have a life of my own, you know."

"Obviously quite an active one. I stopped by last night, and you were gone. In fact, I made several attempts to see you, but you were out quite late."

Ashley felt her temper rising. Just what was he implying? She saw that he was looking at her expectantly, as if awaiting an explanation. "If you must know, I was on an—an errand of mercy."

"You were taking chicken soup to a sick friend, no doubt," he said dryly.

Ashley ignored the sarcasm in his tone. "A family I know was having a problem. The woman who was supposed to stay with the children couldn't get there, so they were home alone."

"And of course you were the only person who could come to their aid."

"I was the one they turned to for help," Ashley replied defensively.

"And they wouldn't be the Shepard children, would they?"

"As a matter of fact, they were. But—"

"I see." Stewart nodded as if that explained a lot.

Ashley bristled with indignation. "That's beside the point. I'd have done the same for anyone who needed me."

"And Mr. Shepard—where was he while you were playing Mary Poppins to his children?"

"He was in Los Angeles. He had to go out of town on business, and the housekeeper was unavoidably detained—"

"It wasn't *your* responsibility to go over there and take over. He should have had the foresight to hire someone who could be depended on, instead of expecting you to step in—"

"A tree fell on the housekeeper's car," Ashley told him, in icy tones. "I believe that's what the insurance companies call an 'act of God.'" Why was she explaining all this to him, anyway? "I don't have to account for my actions or my whereabouts to you. In fact, I don't like the turn this conversation is taking—and I don't like your insinuations."

Stewart instantly assumed a contrite attitude. "Let's not argue," he said in a placating tone. "We have more important matters to discuss."

She opened her mouth to say something, but he went on before she had a chance to speak. "I was hoping to do this in the right atmosphere, over dinner in a nice restaurant, with candles on the table and soft music in the background, but if I don't speak my piece now, I may not get another opportunity. Ever since you got involved with those Shepard children, I'm lucky if I get to see you at all.''

He reached out as if to take her in his arms, but Ashley backed away. His expression registered impatience for just a moment, but then he quickly rearranged his features into a smooth mask. ''It's time we started making plans for our future.''

Ashley's stomach sank. *It's now or never,* a little voice inside her warned. She squared her shoulders and set her chin firmly. ''Stewart, we don't have a future—at least not together.''

Stewart's brows drew together in a frown, as if he resented the interruption. Ashley had the feeling he wished she'd stop behaving like an unreasonable child so they could get things settled. ''Of course we do. You must know how I feel about you—''

She looked directly into his eyes and spoke slowly and distinctly. ''I'm sorry if you've gotten the wrong idea about our relationship, but we do not—I repeat—*do not* have a 'future' together. In fact, there's no point in our continuing to see each other.''

''Surely you don't mean that. You're just upset because of that little tiff we had.''

''I mean *exactly* what I said.'' She suppressed an urge to fling the door open with a dramatic gesture, point a finger, and cry, ''Go!'' like a character in an old-time melodrama. Instead, she opened it calmly and stepped to one side. ''Now please leave,'' she said, in a tone of quiet determination. ''And don't call me again.''

Stewart started to protest, then apparently changed his mind. As he headed out the door, he said, "We'll discuss this another time, when you're in a more reasonable frame of mind."

Ashley opened her mouth to deliver a blistering tirade, but she found herself unable to utter a word. His smug assumption that she was merely being childish and temperamental and would soon come to her senses left her speechless with indignation.

Although it would have satisfied something inside her to slam the door after him with window-rattling force, she managed to keep her emotions under control. Quietly she closed it after him, then leaned against it. Her knees felt weak, and her insides were churning.

She scooped Bridget up and rubbed her cheek against the soft fur. "Under the circumstances, I think that went about as well as could be expected, don't you?" she said in a shaky voice.

Chapter Seven

Ashley's reflection looked back at her with satisfaction. The gently clinging lines of her dress emphasized her soft curves, and its pale blue-green hue enhanced her delicate coloring. It had been several months since she'd had a date with anyone but Stewart—she hadn't realized how much he'd monopolized her time lately—and it was kind of exciting to be dressing up for someone else.

But this wasn't a *date*, she reminded herself. Just because Mike Shepard had asked her to dinner, that didn't mean he was—well, romantically inclined toward her. His invitation certainly hadn't indicated anything except a desire to show his gratitude to her for looking after his children.

"I really appreciate what you did for the kids," he'd said when he'd called her. "Won't you let me thank you by treating you to dinner? I realize that's small payment, but it's the least I can do."

"Oh, but that's not necessary," she'd protested, quelling the unexpected surge of excitement that shot through her at the thought of spending an evening in

Mike's company. She wouldn't want him to take her to dinner because he felt he *owed* her something.

"Please?" He sounded almost wistful, as if he'd be disappointed if she turned him down. When he put it that way, how could she refuse?

Ashley wondered if the blue-green dress might be a bit much, if it might give the impression that she was reading more than was intended into a simple thank-you dinner. But the pronounced glimmer of appreciation in his eyes when he came to pick her up told her she was dressed exactly right.

"By the way, who's looking after the children tonight?" she asked as he escorted her to his car.

"Mrs. Jackson," he replied.

"Why, I thought she'd need a week or two, at least, to recover from her ordeal."

"That's what I thought, too, but she's a pretty tough lady and feels a real obligation to the kids. The insurance company authorized a rental car for her while the claim on her car is being settled, so she was back on the job as soon as she had transportation again."

As Mike explained this, Mrs. Jackson's standing went up several points in Ashley's estimation. She was ashamed of all the unkind thoughts she'd had about the housekeeper the night she'd found the children alone.

She looks so pretty, Mike thought when Ashley was seated across the table from him in the restaurant. He'd been afraid she was going to turn down his dinner invitation. After all, his approach—that he wanted to repay her—hadn't been exactly inspired.

He supposed he could have just come right out and admitted he wanted to see her again. But she was so dedicated to her work that she might feel it wasn't professional to socialize with the parents of her students, or something of the sort. And they'd already gotten off to a bad start, what with his mistaking her for the housekeeper and barking orders at her. And then at that conference at school, he'd compounded the problem by taking offense at an innocent remark she'd made and stalking off in a huff. He'd hoped if he could convince her to have dinner with him, she might begin to see him in a different light.

"I heard about something I think may be just right for Brandon," Ashley said. "A local little-theater group—the Tacoma Players—is sponsoring a series of theater-arts classes for children. It covers everything from acting and playwriting to stage makeup and set design. At the end of the course the students stage their own original production at various parks throughout the summer."

"Hey, that sounds like it would be right up Brandon's alley. He's always making up adventures, and then he cons his sisters into helping him act them out. Jilly will go along with anything, but Sara won't act in his plays unless she gets to be a princess. His latest effort was a space epic, with the hero defending civilization against aliens from another galaxy, and he had a tough time figuring out how to work a princess into the plot."

Ashley's low, silvery laugh rang out like chimes. Mike enjoyed the sound of it so much he almost lost the thread of her words as she went on to say, "I'm glad you like the idea. I'll get all the information for you. I think something like this may be just what he needs to channel his creativity in the right direction.''

Mike was somewhat relieved when the waiter arrived just then to take their orders. As much as he cared about his young charges, when he was in the company of someone as attractive as Ashley, he was sure they could find more meaningful topics of conversation.

In an effort to forestall any further discussion of the children for the time being, as soon as the waiter had gone he asked, ''What do you do when you're not guiding kids like Brandon back onto the straight and narrow?''

Ashley seemed a little surprised by his question.

''You must have hobbies and interests outside of your job,'' he prompted. ''You've spent the night in my robe, and I don't even know know what your favorite color is, or what you do for relaxation, or the name of your all-time favorite old movie.''

Ashley colored slightly at the mention of his robe as she recalled the dreams the scent of his after-shave clinging to it had evoked. ''Blue,'' she murmured. ''Listen to music, play tennis, read. *Dr. Zhivago*. How about you?''

Mike found himself gazing at the little dimple that played around the corner of her mouth. Although he was utterly charmed by the way it kept appearing and disappearing, he found that focusing on it was playing havoc with his powers of concentration. ''What? Oh— green. Jogging and handball. *The Right Stuff*. Not that I wouldn't enjoy seeing *Dr. Zhivago*,'' he added hastily. "A theater in Seattle is running a classic-film festival next month, and I think that's one of the movies on the list. If you'd like, we could drive up and see it together."

Now the dimple stopped playing hide-and-seek and appeared full-blown as she replied, "I'd love to!"

Mike managed to pull his gaze away from that dimple before he completely lost his train of thought and started blathering like an idiot. "Great. I'll find out when *Dr. Zhivago* is playing and give you a call."

Now that the ice had been broken, they seemed to have little trouble finding topics of conversation. Over dinner they discovered a mutual interest in the Beatles and a marked difference of opinion concerning computer colorization of old movies. This last subject brought forth a friendly but heated debate as they lingered over after-dinner coffee.

"Colorizing a classic film is a desecration, like tampering with a work of art," Ashley maintained. "Would you think it was all right to alter the Mona Lisa?"

"It's not the same principle," Mike argued. "Colorizing a movie just makes it more lifelike. Real life isn't in black and white."

Finally, laughing, they agreed to drop the subject, since neither was willing to give in.

By now the waiter was starting to direct pointed looks their way. "The dining room will be closing in fifteen minutes," he informed them with restrained tact when he came by to ask if they needed anything else.

"I have a feeling we've worn out our welcome," Ashley said in a stage whisper.

Mike felt a pang of disappointment. He wasn't ready for the evening to end yet.

"Perhaps you'd like to go next door to our lounge," the waiter suggested. "It stays open until two, and there's a dance floor."

"What do you say we give it a try?" Mike suggested to Ashley. "It's too early to call it a night."

"I say that's a terrific idea," she replied.

The lounge was crowded and noisy. A combo on a platform in one corner was just starting to play a slow number as they entered.

"Shall we give it a whirl?" he asked. At her nod, they threaded their way through the other couples onto the dance floor.

She fit into his arms perfectly, as if that were exactly where she was meant to be. The top of her head came to just below his chin, and her body next to his was soft and warm.

With so many couples around them, they could do little except move their feet slightly and sway gently in time to the music. That was fine with Mike. He would have been content to hold her this way forever, to inhale the subtle scent of cologne that surrounded her and to feel her heart beating against his chest.

All too soon the music ended and the combo swung into a lively rock tune. Mike tried to ask Ashley if she wanted to dance this one, but it was difficult to make himself heard over the loud music, so he simply raised his eyebrows in a questioning expression. She replied with a smile and a nod.

This sort of dancing, with arms flailing and bodies gyrating to a primitive beat, wasn't nearly as pleasant as the kind that called for close physical contact with his partner, Mike thought. Still, he had to admit that the high color in Ashley's cheeks and the sparkle in her eyes, from the vigorous exertion, made her even more attractive.

When they left the lounge, Ashley was surprised to discover that it was after one o'clock. She'd expected to be home by ten or so, after a quiet dinner and some polite conversation, mostly about Brandon and the girls. Instead, they'd danced far into the night, laughing and joking, and she'd had a thoroughly delightful time.

Nothing in Mike's manner had given any indication that he'd only asked her to dinner because he felt he owed her a favor. He'd been attentive, witty, fun to be with. In fact, she hadn't enjoyed herself so much in ages.

When they reached Ashley's apartment, Mike insisted on seeing her all the way to her door, despite her protests that it really wasn't necessary. As they walked through the semidarkness of the parking lot, he put a hand under her elbow when they came to a curbing or to guide her around a rough spot, and the light contact sent little jolts of electricity up her arm.

The entire evening had turned out so different from what she'd expected, she wondered if she was in for any more surprises. Would Mike try to kiss her good night? And, more to the point, would she let him? Not that a kiss was any big deal, she told herself. Like the old song said, *A kiss is just a kiss. . . .* It needn't be any more than a gesture of affection between two people who had shared an enjoyable time together.

Still, wouldn't it make for some uncomfortable situations the next time they had a conference about Brandon or encountered each other at Parents' Night or some other school function? By the time they reached her door, she'd convinced herself that a courteous handshake, along with a *Thank you for a pleasant evening,* would be more fitting.

She turned to face Mike, but before she could voice the polite phrase, she saw something flare in his eyes as he stood looking down at her. All at once her good intentions were forgotten. She was disconcertingly aware of his closeness, of the tangy aroma of his aftershave and the aura of masculinity that emanated from him.

There was no doubt now that he intended to kiss her. The question of whether she was going to let him was purely academic, since she knew she was powerless to resist the subtle magnetism that had sprung up between them. Her entire being tingled with a delicious kind of tension as she simply waited.

A kiss is just a kiss. . . . The phrase kept echoing in the back of her mind as Mike pulled her close and lowered his head. When his lips met hers, all her senses seemed to leap to sudden, vibrant life. . . .

She was caught off guard by the whirlpool of unexpected sensations that took control of her. Her whole world spun dizzily as an incredible sweetness flooded her, leaving her weak and trembling, as if she were melting inside.

Almost of their own volition, her arms crept up around him as she returned his kiss unreservedly. A subtle, barely perceptible change in the pressure of his lips on hers told her he had sensed her surrender.

Ashley wasn't sure how long they stood there in each other's arms—time had lost its meaning. It wasn't until the lights of a car, pulling into the parking lot, shone on them that they drew apart.

"I—ah—" What was it she'd intended to say to him before his kiss had driven all rational thought from her mind? Something about, *A pleasant evening.* . . .

She suppressed an almost hysterical desire to giggle. That was like describing the eruption of Mt. Saint Helens as a minor disturbance.

Mike seemed equally at a loss for words. He appeared to be as shaken by the force of the attraction between them as she was. He put out a tentative hand, then withdrew it, as if he were afraid if he touched her, he might cause sparks to fly.

"I'll call you—soon," he finally got out.

Ashley still hadn't found her voice. With her heart thudding erratically and her breath coming in little gasps, she could only nod as he turned and went down the steps. By the time she was able to quiet her soaring emotions, he had disappeared into the darkness.

Chapter Eight

The sudden jangling of the phone sent a jolt of irritation through Ashley. "It's probably Stewart," she said to Bridget, who was napping in her lap. Since that day she'd told him she didn't want to see him anymore, he'd called several times to see if she'd "come to her senses."

She was tempted to let the answering machine take the call, but she told herself she was being ridiculous. She couldn't go on not answering her telephone indefinitely, just to avoid talking to Stewart. With a resigned sigh she put Bridget off her lap and stood up.

Bridget expressed her displeasure at being ousted from her comfortable spot. "Sorry, kitty," Ashley murmured. Steeling herself, she picked up the phone and said a cautious, "Hello?"

"Ashley?" Mike's deep, rich tones came over the line. "I'm glad I caught you at home."

She felt almost limp with relief that it wasn't Stewart. Or maybe that sudden weakness, that feeling that her bones were turning to jelly, was caused by hearing Mike's voice again.

"The kids just had a terrific idea," he went on, "so

terrific that I'm sorry *I* didn't think of it. I promised them I'd take them up to the Space Needle—they've never been there. We're planning to make a day of it, and they suggested we ask you to go along. We're hoping you can join us.''

Ashley's heart leaped at the prospect of spending an entire day in Mike's company, then settled back down as she reminded herself that it had been the children's idea to ask her. But he *had* said he was sorry *he* hadn't thought of it—

While she wavered back and forth, he apparently misinterpreted her hesitation. "I—ah—guess it was pretty short notice. You probably already have plans for the day.''

"No," she said, almost too quickly. "I mean no, I don't have plans. And yes, I'd love to go.''

"Great." She could almost hear the grin in his voice. "We'll pick you up in about an hour.''

"What do you think I should wear?'' she asked Bridget, who sat on her bed, watching her through half-closed eyes as she surveyed her wardrobe. "I need something comfortable enough for a day of sight-seeing, but that will still. . . .'' Her words trailed off as she considered, then rejected several possibilities. This one was too casual . . . that one not casual enough . . . another simply didn't *do* anything. . . .

What she was really looking for, she admitted to herself, was something that would make Mike sit up and take notice.

Finally she hit on the right combination, a soft, loose-fitting pink knit shirt that clung gently to her curves, worn with her favorite stone-washed denim jeans. A pair of white canvas shoes completed the outfit. *Not bad,* she thought, examining her image in the mirror.

Glancing out the window, she was surprised to see Mike and the children pulling into the parking lot in a light-blue sedan that had an air of reliability about it. When the doorbell rang, she answered it with what she realized was probably unladylike eagerness. She told herself it was just that she knew the children would be impatient to get going and she didn't want to keep them waiting.

"What happened to Little Red?" she asked as Mike escorted her to the car.

"You mean the Maserati? It's home in the garage. It's not very practical for a family man—we couldn't even all ride in it at the same time—so I bought this. I'm looking for a buyer for the Maserati."

The children greeted her as if she were a long-lost friend. They were all eager to share the latest events in their lives with her, and all the way to Seattle they chattered amiably. Jilly had a new "best friend" named Trish, Sara's Girl Scout troop was planning an overnight camp-out, and Brandon was now enrolled in a theater-arts class.

"And guess what, Ashley!" Brandon said. "We're gonna put on plays in some of the parks this summer."

"You don't waste any time, do you?" Ashley commented to Mike with a little smile. She had just called him last week with the information she'd promised.

"Hey, I don't let any grass grow under my feet," Mike replied. "It's a good thing too. There was only one opening left, and the class started this week. Even though he's only gone to one session, he's pretty excited about it. That was a great idea you had.'' He reached over to grasp her hand and give it a gentle squeeze, as if to say *Thank you.*

The gesture didn't go unnoticed by the three children in the backseat, who were leaning as far forward as their seat belts would allow. Ashley heard Jilly's delighted giggle, and in the rearview mirror she could see the knowing look that passed between Sara and Brandon.

''What are your plans for the summer?'' she asked in an attempt to forestall any embarrassing comments. ''You know, school will be out in a few weeks.''

''Trish and I promised each other we'll play together *every single day*,'' Jilly said.

''I'm going to read all of the Beezus and Ramona Quimby books,'' Sara put in. ''I've already read the first two.''

Brandon made a choking sound that indicated his opinion of Sara's choice of summer entertainment. ''Not me, boy. I'm not gonna spend my summer reading *books*. I'm—''

His words broke off as the Seattle skyline came into view. ''Hey, look, there's the Space Needle!'' he exclaimed. ''Wow, it looks just like it does in the pictures!''

But as they left the freeway and Mike maneuvered the car through the crowded Seattle streets, even the usually irrepressible Brandon fell silent. Once they were out of the car and walking toward the Seattle Center, he craned his neck to watch an elevator making its swift ascent up the outside of the Space Needle, while another made its way down. The structure looked even taller up close than it had from the freeway.

By the time Mike bought their tickets, an elevator was ready to leave, and in no time they were being whisked upward. "Awesome," Brandon was heard to murmur under his breath as the ground fell away beneath them.

When they reached the multiwindowed, circular observation deck, the childred rushed out of the elevator, eager to see everything. Sara took Jilly by the hand and patiently helped identify the points of interest, while explaining to her that the Space Needle was six hundred and seven feet high and that it had been built for the Seattle World's Fair in 1962.

Brandon rushed from one side of the deck to the other, unable to make up his mind whether to watch the Victoria Clipper heading out across Puget Sound or a floatplane landing on Lake Union.

Ashley and Mike strolled along at a more leisurely pace, admiring the view. Off to the east the Cascade Range was silhouetted against the sky, a spectacular Mt. Rainier reigning supreme over the smaller peaks. To the west the Olympics faded off into the distance. When Mike casually reached for Ashley's hand and held it, he couldn't help thinking how it felt as if it belonged there—just as she had seemed to belong in his arms.

Except for that one evening with Ashley, he hadn't dated since he'd taken over the care of the kids. Of course, before Mrs. Jackson had come to work for him, he hadn't had any choice. Without someone dependable to look after the kids, his social life had ground to a halt.

Not that he'd really minded. He'd never considered himself much of a ladies' man, anyway, despite the fact that his coworkers and acquaintances were always inviting him to some kind of function, with the intention of pairing him off with a sister, or a wife's best friend, or whatever. Sometimes he wondered why these well-meaning matchmakers couldn't just leave a guy alone. It was a relief to have a handy, ready-made excuse for turning down these invitations.

But that was before he'd met Ashley. He found that he was drawn to her as he'd never been drawn to another woman. He was strangely hesitant about acting on his feelings, though. When she'd called to give him the information about the theater-arts class, he'd wanted to ask if he could see her again, but somehow he hadn't been able to make himself say the words. Several times since then he'd reached for the phone to call her and then had withdrawn his hand. Even though she'd gone out with him once, he couldn't help wondering if she might be hesitant about getting involved with a man who had three children to raise. Did he even have the right to ask her to?

Be realistic, man, his common sense had told him. He already had his hands full. The last thing he needed was a romantic entanglement. But although he'd recounted the many reasons he'd be better off to let well enough alone, all his good intentions had flown right out the window when the kids had suggested they invite Ashley to go to the Space Needle with them. She was the children's friend, too, he reminded himself, and that put everything in a different light. It wouldn't be fair to deprive them of her company. He felt downright virtuous as he picked up the phone to call her. After all, he was doing this for the kids, wasn't he?

Sure, a little voice inside him said. *Just who do you think you're kidding?*

So now here she was by his side, her hand in his, and it felt so *right.*

As they circled the deck, they met up with Sara and Jilly coming from the other direction. "Did you know the Pacific Science Center is right next to the Space Needle?" Sara informed them. "You can see it from up here. Do you think we could go there after we leave here? My teacher says it's very educational."

"It's up to Ashley." Mike glanced over at her. "Are you in a hurry to get back?"

"No, I have all the time in the world. And I love the Science Center."

"Then it's settled. That's next on our agenda."

Brandon appeared in time to hear this exchange. "The *Science Center,*" he echoed, in the tone of one facing an ordeal. "That sounds bo-ring."

But he was outvoted, so when the little group had seen all the Space Needle had to offer, they headed for the Science Center. In spite of his cool reception to the idea, Brandon was awed by the hands-on exhibits, the turn-of-the-century Native American dwelling, and the laser show. "Wow, that was the most fun place I ever went to!" he exclaimed as they came back out into the sunlight.

The next order of business was getting something to eat. Since they couldn't agree on what they were in the mood for, Mike suggested they go to the Food Fair in the Center House, so they could all have something different. Once there, Brandon went in search of a pizza stand where he could get his favorite, pepperoni pizza. Mike and Jilly decided on hot dogs, and Ashley and Sara opted for Chinese food.

When they were finally all gathered around a table with their various dishes before them, Brandon asked, "You're coming to one of the plays my theater-arts class is putting on, aren't you, Ashley? They don't start until after school is out, so you probably won't be very busy."

"Now, you can't just assume that once vacation starts Ashley will have unlimited free time and will be at your beck and call," Mike cautioned. "I'm sure she has plans of her own." Although the thought of monopolizing *all* of Ashley's free time was definitely appealing, he didn't want to overwhelm her.

"As a matter of fact, I'm going to Wenatchee for my sister's wedding a few weeks after school's out, and I'm going to be tutoring several students over the summer, but I won't be busy every minute. I promise I'll find time to come to your play. I wouldn't miss it."

Brandon's expression of relief wasn't lost on Mike. It was obvious that Ashley's presence at his acting debut meant a great deal to the boy. Mike had noticed other little signs, also, that Ashley was becoming an important figure in his kids' lives—the trusting way Jilly slipped her hand into Ashley's when they were walking along, the girlish exchanges between Ashley and Sara, as if they were contemporaries. He sensed that it meant a lot to a girl Sara's age to have an older friend or confidante—something along the lines of a big sister or a favorite aunt—and Ashley obviously fulfilled that role for her.

It was early evening when they finally started home. At the beginning of the drive back, the children chattered excitedly about everything they had seen and done today, but by the time they reached Tacoma, Jilly's head was bobbing sleepily, and even Sara and Brandon were winding down.

"You kids wait here," Mike said, pulling up in front of Ashley's apartment building. "I'll be right back."

"I'm glad you came with us today," Mike said as he and Ashley said their good-byes outside her door. "The kids really enjoyed having you along." He winced inwardly as he realized how that sounded. Doggone it, why was he having such a hard time saying what was in his heart? Maybe it was because he was aware that all three children had suddenly become wide-awake and were practically hanging out the car window.

"I'm glad you asked me." Ashley tilted her face up to his, and that dimple appeared briefly, like sunshine peeking out from behind a cloud. "I hope you'll invite me along again sometime—when you're taking the children on another outing."

Was she teasing him? He wasn't sure, but if she was, he deserved it.

"We—ah—don't have to wait until I'm taking the kids someplace. We could. . . ." His words trailed off as he found himself looking into her eyes. In the gathering twilight they seemed dark and mysterious, as if they were beckoning to him. A man could get lost in them. . . .

With a real effort he pulled his glance away, and his eyes traveled on down to her delicately tinted lips. They looked so warm and inviting, so —so *kissable*. His senses recalled how they had felt under his, and he instinctively lowered his head toward hers. . . .

A muffled giggle brought him back to reality. Glancing around toward the car, he saw that the kids were watching with unabashed interest. He thought he could hear faint groans of disappointment coming from their direction as he straightened up and pulled away from Ashley.

"I'll call you—very soon," he murmured in a tone too low for the kids to hear before he turned and walked away.

From the car, he watched until Ashley was safely inside the building. As he started the engine and put the car into gear, he was thinking that he definitely intended to explore this new relationship. He'd prefer to do it without an audience, though.

Chapter Nine

Ashley closed the folder and put it with the others in a neat pile on the corner of her desk. It was about time for a break. Tomorrow was the last day of school, and she'd been working steadily for the last few hours, making sure all her records were up to date before vacation started.

Standing up, she twisted her head from side to side to work some of the kinks out of her neck and shoulders. She reached for the coffeepot, then changed her mind. She'd go down to the teachers' lounge for coffee instead. She needed to get out of the office for a little while.

The building had a deserted air. Usually the halls of Soundview Academy were a beehive of activity even between classes, with students delivering attendance records to the office or running other errands, or entire classes on their way to the library or a field trip. Right now an end-of-the-school-year assembly was taking place in the auditorium, though, so the halls were empty.

The teachers' lounge, too, was unoccupied. Most of the staff, of course, would also be at the assembly.

She would have been there herself, but she wanted to start her vacation without the specter of any unfinished duties hanging over her.

After a leisurely cup of coffee, Ashley started back to her office, feeling refreshed and ready to tackle the rest of her stack of paperwork. She was just rounding the last corner when she almost collided with a smaller figure coming from the other direction.

"Brandon! Why aren't you at the assembly?" she asked. "All the students are supposed to be there."

A wary look came into Brandon's eyes as he backed away. "I—I—ah—"

Now what was the little scamp up to? Ashley wondered. Had he simply gotten bored with the assembly and managed to slip away? Well, that wasn't really such a terrible offense. On a warm spring day like this one, she understood how difficult it was for a lively child like Brandon to sit quietly.

Still, she supposed it was her duty to reprimand him. If he were allowed to sneak out of assembly whenever he took a notion, pretty soon they'd have students wandering all over the building unsupervised.

But before she could say anything to him, she heard the jangle of her office phone. She considered just letting it ring while she turned her attention to getting Brandon sent back to where he belonged. But it might be important, she thought. She'd find out who it was and either return the call or put the caller on hold.

"I'll be right back to talk to you," she said to Brandon as she rushed off to answer her phone.

It turned out to be one of the administrators, who wanted to discuss her budget for the coming school year. Several times Ashley tried to break in long enough to say, "Look, I'm right in the middle of something. Could we talk about this later?" but she wasn't able to get a word in.

By the time she finally got off the phone, she could hear the students on their way out for recess, so she knew the assembly was over. She glanced out into the hallway, but Brandon was nowhere in sight. Well, she couldn't really blame him. She'd been on the phone for so long, he probably assumed she'd forgotten about him. After recess she'd check to make sure he'd gone back to his class.

As she resumed her paperwork, it crossed her mind that a short time ago the idea of Brandon roaming the empty halls with no supervision would have sent cold chills through her. To everyone's relief, his behavior had improved considerably in just a few weeks. Since Mike had enrolled him in that theater-arts program, he seemed almost a different child. Oh, he still had that same impish charm that made it difficult to become really angry with him, but he was learning to put his more imaginative impulses to better use.

Mike had told her, the last time she'd spoken to him on the phone, that the change in his nephew was remarkable. "You can't imagine what a load has been taken off my mind," he'd said, "now that I'm not constantly worried about what kind of trouble Brandon will get into next."

Ashley was delighted to hear that the boy had "seen the error of his ways," and that things were going well in the Shepard household now.

"Things" seemed to be going well on other counts,

too, she thought with a little smile. Mike had called her a couple of times, to update her on Brandon's progress and to remind her they had a date to see *Dr. Zhivago*. The warmth in his tone had left no doubt in Ashley's mind that he was looking forward to seeing her again. The knowledge sent a little glow of pleasure through her.

Lately she found that thoughts of Mike were occupying a good deal of her waking hours—and some of her dreams as well. She'd even allowed herself to fantasize just a little, to imagine what it would be like to be married to him.

She chided herself for being overly romantic. After all, she barely knew him. Just because he'd invited her to go along on a family outing and taken her to dinner once (and kissed her good night very thoroughly, a little voice in the back of her consciousness put in), that didn't imply a lifelong commitment, for goodness' sake.

But love doesn't have a timetable. Now where had *that* thought come from? That same insistent little voice reminded her that although she'd dated Stewart for several months, he had never awakened any romantic feelings in her. Yet, just remembering the feeling of being in Mike's arms, of his lips on hers, was enough to send her senses reeling. . . .

She could feel a flush of crimson staining her cheeks as her reverie was interrupted by a light tap at the door. ''Come in,'' she called, attempting to bring her thoughts under control.

Noreen Canfield, the assistant principal, stuck her

head in. "Ashley, would you come down to the science room? There's something I think you should see."

"Sure, I'll be right there," she replied. "Just let me finish jotting down a few notes in this file."

As she made her way to Duane Spaulding's classroom a few minutes later, she wondered what was so important down there. Had one of his classes conducted an especially interesting experiment and wanted to show it off to someone? They must have known she'd be an appreciative audience. She always tried to be interested in what the students were doing.

When she reached the science room, she found Noreen waiting for her, along with Duane and the principal, Lester Applegate. "Hi," she greeted them, stepping into the room. "What's up. . . ."

Her voice trailed off as she looked about the room in stunned disbelief. She could do nothing but gasp at the scene of destruction that met her eyes.

Chairs and tables were overturned. Books and papers were strewn around the room. A terrarium and several potted plants on the window shelf had been destroyed, the plants pulled up by the roots and dirt and gravel spread about. There was more damage, but Ashley's shocked senses couldn't take it all in at once.

"What—who—" she stammered.

"It must have been done while everyone was at the assembly," Duane explained, shaking his head. "I was just as stunned as you are when I came back and found this mess." He was a soft-spoken, middle-aged man whose primary aim in life was to impart to his students his deep reverence for science. He looked saddened and bewildered, rather than angry, as he surveyed the devastation.

"Have the police been called?" Ashley asked.

"No, we prefer to handle this ourselves, if possible," Lester replied. His sandy, thinning hair was disarranged, as if he'd run a hand through it in frustration.

"Do you have any idea who could have done such a terrible thing?"

"That's why we sent for you," he replied. "We were hoping you might be able to offer some help, since you didn't go to the assembly. Did you notice anyone in this part of the building who didn't belong here?"

"Only Brandon." The words escaped Ashley before she had time to weigh them.

Lester's brows drew together in a frown. "Brandon Shepard? I might have known he'd be responsible for this. Well, he's gone too far this time."

Ashley was appalled that her innocent remark was being taken as an accusation against Brandon. "But we don't know for sure that he did it," she pointed out.

Lester gave her a long-suffering look. "You just said he was in the vicinity." Ashley knew the principal usually bent over backward to be fair to his students, but he had the air of a man who had reached the end of his patience.

"That doesn't necessarily make Brandon the guilty party," she protested.

"If it were any other child, I'd be inclined to agree, but you have to admit he doesn't have a very good track record. He's been in trouble of one kind or another from the day he came to Soundview.''

"But those were just pranks. Brandon wouldn't do something like this." She glanced around the room at the destruction. "He may be mischievous and high-spirited, but he's never been malicious."

"Look, let's ask Brandon if he has some valid reason for why he was roaming around the building when he should have been at assembly," Noreen put in, in a conciliatory tone. "Why don't I go find him, and we'll see what he has to say?"

"Well, I suppose he has a right to tell his side of it," Lester grudgingly agreed, although his expression clearly indicated he had no doubt that he had his culprit. "I'll see you in my office in a little while."

"I think I'll stay here," Duane said. "My students will be coming in from recess any minute, and I'd rather they didn't see the classroom until I've had a chance to at least straighten up some of the mess."

Brandon seemed his usual happy-go-lucky self when Noreen ushered him into Lester's office a little while later. Ashley watched him closely for any sign that he had something to hide, but his expression displayed only a good-natured curiosity about why he had been summoned.

She reminded herself he *had* looked—well, almost guilty when she'd encountered him in the hall earlier. Still, her instincts told her he would never have done anything like that.

"I'll get right to the point," Lester said. "Somebody vandalized the science room during assembly. We have reason to think you—ah—may be able to tell us something about who did it.''

"Vandalized the science room,'' Brandon echoed. "You mean—like *trashed* it?'' His face went white under his freckles. "You don't think it was *me*, do you? I know sometimes I—I do stuff I shouldn't, but I wouldn't *wreck* things.''

"Then maybe you'd like to explain why you were wandering about the halls when you should have been at the assembly.''

Brandon's brow furrowed. "I—I had something I needed to do in the art room. Mrs. Freeman gave me permission to miss the assembly.''

"Why would she do that?'' Lester demanded sharply.

"It was because I'm working on a—a project. I wanted to paint it now and give it time to dry so I can put another coat on it before I go home today. See, I got some paint on me.'' He pointed to a smudge of bright green on his arm.

"What was the big rush, that you had to miss assembly in order to finish this—this project?''

Brandon shoved his hands into his pockets and ducked his head. Even Ashley had to admit that he looked like someone who knew he'd been caught red-handed. Lester's expression was triumphant.

"Now you've spoiled the surprise,'' Brandon mumbled. "I'm making a bookshelf—it's a present for Miss Kendall. I wanted to finish painting it today because tomorrow's the last day of school.''

"Ohhh.'' The single word escaped Ashley. Her heart went out to the boy, who had merely wanted to do something nice for her and now was having to defend his actions.

Lester's frown deepened. His expression left no doubt that he suspected this was something Brandon had manufactured on the spur of the moment, to get himself out of hot water.

"If Harriet gave him permission to be in another part of the building during assembly, that should be easy enough to verify," Noreen put in, in an attempt to ease the tense situation.

"Even if he's telling the truth about having permission to miss assembly—and we can check on that, of course—that still doesn't clear him," Lester pointed out. "He would have had ample time to paint his bookshelf and still get to the science room." He fixed Brandon with a stern look. "This is more serious than your past pranks. I think I'd better call your uncle in for a talk."

"But I didn't *do* it," Brandon protested.

Ashley felt a surge of protectiveness toward the boy as his thin shoulders slumped in defeat, but she restrained the urge to rush to him. She sensed he wouldn't appreciate a display of sympathy in front of Lester and Noreen. She felt compelled to speak up in his defense, however. "Surely he isn't the only student in the entire school who can't account for where he was at that time."

"But he's the only one we *know* was roaming around the hallways then. I'm not saying it was definitely Brandon, but it's something we at least have to take a closer look at." Lester reached for the telephone on his desk. "Brandon, you may return to your class now.

And go straight there,'' he admonished. ''Don't stop along the way.''

The atmosphere in the small office was tense. ''What I don't understand,'' Mike was saying in a tightly controlled voice, ''is why, out of all the students at Soundview, Brandon is the one you're zeroing in on.'' He was already annoyed about having been called away from his work to come and talk to the principal, and hearing his nephew accused of wanton vandalism did nothing to improve his mood. ''What does Brandon have to say about this?'' he asked.

Lester cleared his throat nervously. ''He denies it, of course, but—''

''If Brandon says he didn't do it, that's good enough for me.'' Mike stood up, as if to indicate the meeting was over. He crossed the room in a few short strides, then turned around when he reached the door. Almost as an afterthought he asked, ''Incidentally, how did you happen to come up with Brandon as your culprit?''

''Now, now. We haven't accused him of anything yet.'' Lester looked decidedly uncomfortable. ''But he *is* the only student we can definitely place in the vicinity of the science room during that time. I know that in itself isn't incriminating, but in view of his *past record. . . .*'' He emphasized the last two words before letting his voice trail off.

Mike nodded slightly, as if this were no more than he'd expected. ''I see. So you have him tried and convicted on purely circumstantial evidence, and even that evidence is pretty shaky. How do you *know* he was near the science room?''

"There's no doubt about that aspect of the situation. Miss Kendall saw him there. She brought it to our attention shortly after the vandalism was discovered."

Mike paused with his hand on the doorknob, and his eyes met Ashley's. For just a second she caught a look of hurt and disappointment on his face before his expression became a granite mask. An icy chill ran through her and settled in the pit of her stomach as she realized he blamed *her* because his nephew was under suspicion.

"I—I didn't *accuse* Brandon," she stammered. "All I said was that he was in the hallway—"

"And of course that automatically makes him guilty. I know Brandon has had some behavior problems, but lately he's really been trying to get his act together. I thought you, of all people, would be willing to give him a chance, but I see you're just like everyone else— unable to overlook his past mistakes." With that, he turned and left the room.

The silence hung in the air like a tangible thing. Lester was the first to speak. "Maybe we did jump the gun a bit in calling in Mr. Shepard before we had any definite proof that it was Brandon, but I felt he should know that his nephew was a possible suspect."

"So what happens now?" Ashley asked through lips that felt stiff.

Lester shook his head as if he wished the whole problem would just disappear. "Brandon should be made to make some kind of restitution, but we can't do much until more evidence turns up."

Ashley wanted to point out that it was just possible Brandon *was* innocent. She had such a lump in her throat, though, she was afraid that if she tried to speak, she might embarrass herself by bursting into tears. Finally she managed to stammer something about having things she had to finish and escaped to the privacy of her office.

She had difficulty keeping her mind on her work the rest of the day. Every time she tried to concentrate, Mike's face appeared before her. Tension knotted painfully inside her as she recalled the stern line of his mouth and the cold aloofness in his eyes.

Surely he couldn't think she'd *meant* to implicate Brandon. What had her exact words been when Lester asked if she'd noticed anyone in this part of the building? "Only Brandon," she'd replied, never dreaming Lester would misinterpret that to mean she was naming Brandon as the guilty party.

Perhaps if she called Mike. . . . She couldn't right now, of course. He'd be on his way back to the plant. Besides, it might be a good idea if she gave him a little time for his anger to dissipate. She'd give him a call this evening. Once she explained what had actually taken place, there was no reason why he'd stay angry over what was, after all, just a silly misunderstanding. He was a reasonable man. She felt the pall of depression that had settled over her start to lift.

Half in anticipation, half in dread, Ashley punched out Mike's number that evening. In spite of the pep talk she'd given herself earlier, she couldn't suppress a twinge of apprehension as she waited for him to answer. She kept remembering the cold, hard look he'd given her just before he'd turned and strode from Lester's office. . . .

"Shepard residence."

Her stomach did flip-flops as Mike's voice came over the line. Her carefully prepared little speech deserted her, and for a few seconds her mind went blank.

"Hello? Is anyone there?"

With an effort she pulled herself together. "Mike, this is Ashley. I—ah—I have to talk to you about what happened at school today—"

"It seems you've already said more than enough, haven't you?" His tone was hard and expressionless. "I don't think we have anything to say to each other." There was a click, and the line went dead.

Shock waves ran through Ashley as she stared at the instrument in her hand. A multitude of emotions ran through her, from humiliation and frustration to sudden resentment, as surprise gave way to a rising tide of white-hot anger. Who did he think he was, anyway? She told herself she was fortunate to have found out how stubborn and judgmental he could be, before their relationship went any further.

But it was too late, a little voice inside her said. She was already more than a little in love with him. Or, at least, she'd *thought* she was. But she couldn't really be in love with someone so high-handed and unbending, could she? What she felt for him couldn't be any more than a mere physical attraction.

That was what her common sense told her. But that didn't keep her from crying herself to sleep that night or from having restless, disjointed dreams in which

Mike was striding away from her, his mouth set in a firm, unyielding line and his eyes cold and aloof.

She awoke with a throbbing head and red, swollen eyes. The last thing she felt like doing was going to work, but it was the last day of school, and she had several loose ends to tie up.

It didn't help any that when she arrived at school, she found a message that Lester wanted to see her. In some vague way she blamed him for this whole mess. But that wasn't fair, she knew. This couldn't be easy for him, either. If something was amiss in his school, it was up to him to get to the bottom of it, and even though her instincts told her Brandon was innocent, he *was* the most likely suspect.

When she entered Lester's office, she noticed he looked almost as harried as she felt. Yesterday had been a bad day all around, she thought.

Lester cleared his throat. "There have been some— ah—new developments in that incident involving the science room. I felt you should be one of the first to know."

Was he going to tell her they had proof that Brandon had done it? She waited for him to go on.

"When I talked to Ernie this morning, he recalled seeing two boys hanging around the grounds yesterday," Lester said. Ernie was the school custodian, who usually kept his finger on everything that happened on the premises. "He knew they weren't students here, but he recognized them as living in the neighborhood. He said he thought it was odd that they weren't in school. He was about to tell them to go play somewhere else, but he had to go set up the sound system for the assembly right then. By the time he was finished, the boys were nowhere in sight, so he didn't give it another thought at the time.''

''Why didn't he tell us this when the vandalism was discovered?''

''Ernie left early yesterday—he had to go and take his insurance physical. He didn't know about what had happened in the science room until he came in this morning. When he told me, I called the school these boys go to and found out they both had unexcused absences yesterday.''

''You mean they were skipping school.''

He nodded. ''To make a long story short, when confronted, they admitted they'd sneaked into the science room while nobody was around and vandalized it.''

''But—but why?''

Lester shrugged. ''Who knows? Apparently they were just looking for some trouble to get into. They sneaked into our building, and the science room just happened to be the first room they came to.''

''What happens now?'' Ashley asked. She was having trouble taking all this in.

''The boys' parents have been notified. Since this is a first offense, we've agreed to not press charges if the damage is paid for and the boys help clean up the mess they made.''

''So, now what about Brandon?''

''I've already spoken to him. I explained that we'd found the boys who were responsible, and I told him how sorry I am that he was unjustly accused. He took it very well and didn't seem to have any hard feelings. In some ways, he really is a pretty good kid.''

"And Mr. Shepard—I suppose he's also been told.''

"Oh, yes,'' Lester replied with a grimace. "I called him as soon as I knew.''

One thing about Lester, Ashley thought, was that he wasn't one to shirk his duty, no matter how disagreeable it might be.

"He didn't take it nearly as well as Brandon,'' Lester went on. "Oh, he accepted my apology, but he wasn't exactly cordial. Not that I blame him, after we practically accused his nephew.'' He sighed heavily. "Well, if nothing else came of this whole mess, at least I learned a good lesson about not jumping to conclusions.''

And I learned a thing or two about not giving my heart away too easily, Ashley reflected dismally. Might as well put all thoughts of Mike out of her mind, she told herself. Whatever might have been was over before it had gotten started.

The knowledge left her feeling desolate and empty.

Later that morning Brandon peeked in the open door of Ashley's office.

"Why, hello, Brandon,'' she said, glancing up from her work. "What can I do for you?''

He stepped inside and, with a flourish and a "Ta-da!'' held out an object that consisted of a piece of wood about eighteen inches long, with a shorter piece attached to each end at right angles. It appeared to be held together with enough nails to build an entire house.

"It's a bookshelf,'' he explained.

Touched that he still wanted her to have it, Ashley stood up and came around her desk to accept the offering. "This is one of the nicest things anyone has ever given me," she said, examining it from all angles. And she truly meant it. In spite of the fact that it was rickety and lopsided and painted in a shade of green that could almost be described as fluorescent, she appreciated the devotion that had gone into making it.

She made a little ceremony of clearing a spot for it on the window ledge, where it clashed violently with the soft, muted blue of the drapes and the carefully chosen pictures on either side of the window. Together she and Brandon picked out several books that would set it off to the best advantage, then stood back to admire their handiwork.

When Brandon left Ashley's office, he was beaming happily. *At least Brandon likes me,* she thought as she watched him walk jauntily down the hall, *even if his uncle thinks I'm a traitor.*

Chapter Ten

"Oh, Ashley, I can hardly believe that by tomorrow at this time I'll be married," Jessica said with a sigh. There was a glow about her that gave her a soft, dreamy look. It was the glow of a woman in love.

"And you're going to be the most beautiful bride ever," Ashley assured her sister.

The past few days—ever since Ashley had arrived at her parents' home—had been a whirlwind of parties, luncheons, and other get-togethers. This evening Ashley and Jessica had escaped the round of prewedding festivities for some much needed privacy.

Now they sat facing each other on the twin beds in the room they had shared the whole time they were growing up. Jessica's wedding gown, a confection of creamy satin and frosty lace, shared space in the closet with Ashley's dusty-rose maid-of-honor dress. In front of Ashley on the bed, Bridget was attacking a bit of ribbon from a just-opened wedding present.

Ashley couldn't help a slight twinge of envy at the way her sister's life was so neatly settled. Jessica and Kevin had been in love since high school, and there had never been the slightest doubt in either of their minds that they would eventually marry. What a relief it must be to have your life in order, Ashley thought— to know, beyond a doubt, that you were in love and that you were loved in return. Would she ever know that kind of assurance? she wondered.

"This is the first chance we've had for a good old-fashioned sister-to-sister chat since you got here," Jessica said. "So tell me, what's going on in your life? Is there any special man in the picture?"

Ashley shook her head. "I'm afraid not."

"Honestly?" Jessica looked skeptical.

"Honestly," Ashley asserted. Pulling Bridget onto her lap, she suddenly became very intent on untangling the ribbon that the cat had gotten tangled up in her claws.

"Aha!" Jessica exclaimed dramatically.

"Aha? What does that mean?"

"Don't play games with me. This is your sister, remember? I know that expression—it means there's something you're not telling me. Now *out* with it."

Ashley released Bridget, who immediately became entangled again. "There was someone—I thought there might be something between us," she finally admitted, "but it didn't work out." She tried to indicate, by her offhand manner, that it didn't really matter.

But her sister folded her arms decisively. "Okay, let's hear the rest of the story."

Ashley sighed. She'd hoped she wouldn't be pressed for details, but Jessica's expression made it clear that she wasn't going to let the matter drop. With a little shrug, Ashley decided she might as well give in gracefully. If you couldn't confide in a sister, who *could* you confide in?

"His name is Mike Shepard, and he's an engineer out at Flint. He's the uncle of three of my students. . . ."

She found herself telling Jessica the entire story, from her first visit to the Shepard household to the misunderstanding over the vandalism incident.

"It sounds like you two had something pretty good going for you," Jessica said. "Surely he'll realize he jumped to a wrong conclusion."

"I don't think so. You didn't see his face when he stalked out of Mr. Applegate's office. Or hear his voice when I tried to call and explain that evening—just before he hung up on me."

"Do you love him?" Jessica asked bluntly.

"No—I don't know—" Ashley's words broke off, as she searched the hidden places of her heart. The room became very quiet.

"Yes," she admitted after a long silence. "And I was beginning to think he felt the same way."

"Then don't give up if you honestly feel there's something worth salvaging," Jessica advised.

"It wouldn't work," Ashley insisted. "He's proud and stubborn and independent—and he's fiercely protective of those children."

Jessica mulled this over. "Hmmm. Those sound like pretty good qualities in a man. Oh, not the stubbornness, maybe, but even that can be an asset. Who wants a guy who can be led around by the nose?"

"It doesn't matter, anyway. It was over between us almost before it got started."

"I wouldn't be too sure about that," Jessica replied. "If you love each other, these things have a way of working themselves out."

Ashley couldn't help smiling at her sister's all-knowing tone. "And when did you become such an expert on affairs of the heart?" she teased.

"I *am* almost a married woman," Jessica reminded her with an exaggerated air of superiority. "We know about these things. Besides, I'm older than you, you know," she went on, referring to the year's difference in their ages. "Listen to your big sist—mmmph."

Her words were cut off as the pillow Ashley tossed at her caught her in the face, bringing the serious discussion to an end.

The ceremony the following day was beautiful. Just before the organist struck up the wedding march, a beam of sunshine shot through one of the stained-glass windows, like a benediction on the bride and groom.

As Ashley stood in her place at the front of the church, watching a radiantly happy Jessica float down the aisle, she stole a glance at Kevin. His expression was so full of love for Jessica that Ashley's eyes misted over. Would any man ever look at *her* that way? she wondered.

Would *Mike* ever look at her that way? a little voice inside her amended.

"Don't you see," Stewart was saying, "what an embarrassing position this puts me in?"

Ashley had barely had time to set her suitcase down inside the door and let Bridget out of her traveling cage when the phone rang.

Her first impulse had been to ignore it. After driving for almost three hours, she needed a little time to unwind. But what if it was Mike? What if—after he'd had time to weigh the situation—he'd realized he'd misjudged her and was calling to make amends? For all she knew, he could have been trying to reach her the whole time she'd been in Wenatchee. After a moment or two of indecision, she'd grabbed the phone on the next ring—and regretted it as soon as she heard Stewart's voice. He was calling to remind her that one of his clients had invited them to a cocktail party.

She tried to keep her impatience from being too obvious. "Do you really think it will make any difference to your client whether I'm there or not? Why don't you take someone else?"

"The invitation was extended to both of us, and you *did* accept," he reminded her. "If I show up with some other woman—assuming I could even find someone to go with me on such short notice—my client might begin to have doubts about my dependability. My success as an investment broker depends, a good deal, on my presenting a reliable, stable image, you know. People don't want to entrust their money to someone who doesn't have both feet on the ground."

Ashley felt he was exaggerating. She thought it unlikely that the client and his wife would even remember who Stewart had been with when the two couples had met one evening at a charity auction, shortly before Ashley had made the decision to stop seeing him. After introductions all around and a few moments of casual conversation, the older couple had issued an informal invitation to their upcoming cocktail party. Ashley had forgotten the incident—or when she did think about it, she'd assumed that since she was no longer seeing Stewart, he would find someone else to take or go alone.

"This man is an important business contact," Stewart went on. "I'm sure you wouldn't want to do anything to jeopardize my career."

Ashley sighed heavily. He was playing on her sense of duty. And what was worse—it was working. Since she *had* accepted the invitation and Stewart's client was expecting both of them, she supposed she owed it to him to show up at the party—as long as he fully understood she was only agreeing to this as a favor. Maybe once she did this for him, he'd stop bothering her. If spending one more evening in his company was what it took to get him out of her hair, it was a small price to pay. . . .

As he drove up to the Sheldons' spacious Brown's Point home, overlooking Commencement Bay, Mike was wishing there had been some way of getting out of this shindig. He didn't see any way he could have gracefully refused, though. Jack Sheldon was one of those in the upper echelons at Flint, and an invitation from him was considered an honor.

Maybe once he put in an appearance and stayed long enough to let his host and hostess know he'd been there, he could slip away. Knowing the Sheldons' taste for doing things on a lavish scale, he was sure there would be enough people around that he wouldn't even be missed. He'd never been much for partying to begin with, and lately he had less and less taste for that sort of thing. Maybe he was becoming antisocial, but after that experience with Ashley, he'd rather just spend his free time at home with the kids. There was less chance of being disappointed that way. Ashley's betrayal—for that was how he thought of it—had affected him more than he liked to admit.

No other woman had ever gotten to him the way Ashley had. For a while he'd even allowed himself to believe he might be falling in love with her. Oh, he'd told himself that was crazy—he hardly knew her. People didn't fall in love that quickly. But with the family responsibilities that had been thrust on him so unexpectedly, he had little time for the usual courting rituals, the little "getting to know you," man-woman games others took for granted.

He realized how unromantic that sounded, but he had a feeling that when he met the right woman, she would be more interested in what was in his heart than in the outward trappings of romance.

For a short time he'd allowed himself to hope Ashley might be that woman. He'd sensed an affinity, a certain rapport he'd never experienced with any other woman.

But that episode in the principal's office, when she'd practically accused Brandon of vandalism, had effectively put an end to any fleeting thoughts he might have had that Ashley was the woman for him. Hearing her implicate Brandon, he'd felt as if he'd been punched in the stomach.

He sighed deeply. Sometimes he had the feeling everyone was waiting to swoop down on Brandon and blame him for whatever went wrong. Not that the kid didn't deserve it, in some cases. He'd pulled some pretty wild stunts in the past. But he was really trying to change. Why couldn't people give him a chance? Mike wasn't too surprised that old Applegate had pounced on Brandon as the most likely suspect, but he'd expected Ashley to at least give him the benefit of the doubt.

He'd thought she really cared about Brandon—and about him. . . .

He forced himself to put the whole episode out of his mind. Thinking about it hurt too much. He concentrated his attention on negotiating the twists and turns that led up to the Sheldon residence.

"Good to see you, Mike," Jack Sheldon greeted him as he was shown into the spacious house. "Glad you could make it. My wife is around here someplace. She'll be happy to see you too." He introduced Mike to several people standing nearby and stopped a waiter going by with a tray of drinks.

Mike accepted a glass from the assortment that was being held out to him, without bothering to see what the choices were. It didn't matter much, anyway. As long as he had *something* in his hand, he could wander around and sort of blend in until he could quietly make his exit.

"I've been wanting to tell you what a terrific job you did on that pressurization project," Jack said heartily. "It's great to have such bright young engineers in the company—"

"Uncle Jack, there you are." A curvaceous blonde in a low-cut black dress that left little to the imagination sidled up to the host and linked her arm through his. "Aren't you going to introduce me to your guest?"

Sheldon looked slightly annoyed at the interruption, but he smiled indulgently. "Mike, I'd like you to meet my niece, Valerie."

Mike acknowledged the introduction automatically. He was too busy calculating how soon he could slip out without hurting his host's feelings to pay much attention to the young woman who was giving him the full benefit of her dazzling smile.

"I see my wife trying to get my attention," Sheldon said to Mike. "I'd better go see what she wants." He turned to his niece. "Valerie, would you take care of Mike for me? Take him around to meet people—see that he has whatever he needs."

Mike groaned inwardly as his host turned and walked across the room. The last thing he wanted was to be "taken care of" by Valerie. She had a predatory look in her eyes that made him distinctly uncomfortable.

He managed to make small talk with her until another guest joined them and engaged Valerie in conversation. While her attention was thus occupied, he murmured, "Will you excuse me? I just spotted someone I want to say hello to." With this, he made his way across the room to where he'd seen several of his coworkers.

He chatted briefly with a couple of other engineers from the plant, then moved on to another group nearer to where he'd come in, all the while watching Valerie out of the corner of his eye. Just a few more feet, and he could slip out unnoticed. He set his still-untouched drink down on a nearby table and edged closer to the door.

He was about to make his break when, over the hum of conversation, he heard his host almost at his elbow, welcoming another guest. "Nice to see you, Lattimer. And you brought—" Sheldon's next words were drowned out by a burst of laughter somewhere nearby.

That was a close call, Mike thought, relieved that he hadn't turned around. He'd wait until Sheldon moved on; then he'd slip out the door.

The low rumble of a male voice responded to Sheldon's greeting. Mike paid little attention. He just wanted to be on his way.

But when a feminine voice joined in, he froze. "Thank you so much for inviting us," someone behind him was murmuring in hauntingly familiar tones.

No, it couldn't be, Mike thought. This was ridiculous. He had to get himself under control. He was acting like a lovesick adolescent, allowing every random snatch of overheard conversation to conjure up thoughts of Ashley. Just because her voice had that distinctive, husky, breathless quality. . . .

But just then, when he heard that low, silvery laugh ring out in response to some remark of Sheldon's, he knew he wasn't imagining things. Steeling himself, he turned around slowly.

She looked incredibly lovely as she stood talking to their host. When she smiled at something Sheldon said, bringing that dimple into play, his heart twisted with longing.

Already Ashley was sorry she'd let Stewart talk her into coming to this party. She'd only agreed to accompany him out of a sense of obligation. She hoped he wasn't going to use this as an excuse to try to start things up between them again.

But since she *had* come, she supposed she owed it to him to make a good impression. The least she could do was to circulate and chat with the other guests. Besides, Stewart would be easier to cope with if she kept moving. She didn't want him hanging onto her all evening, as if she were his private property. She turned to glance around the room, looking for a likely prospect to strike up a conversation with.

A soft little gasp of astonishment escaped her as she found herself looking into a pair of familiar brown eyes. Her first thought was that her imagination was playing tricks on her. But Mike was very real. So real that the magnetism radiating from him was as strong as if there were just inches between them, instead of ten feet or so.

Everything around her faded away—the roomful of people, the babble of voices, the soft music in the background. At that moment nothing mattered except that she was standing face-to-face with Mike.

For a fraction of a second, as Mike's eyes met Ashley's, something stirred deep inside him. Caught off guard by the unexpected encounter, he felt a yearning so strong it was almost a physical pain. If he'd followed his instincts, he'd have closed the distance between them in just a few strides. But in that moment of hesitation, the events of their last meeting superimposed themselves over his vision. With an effort he suppressed the feelings that had taken him by surprise. Forcing his gaze away from Ashley's, he broke eye contact.

Who was that guy she was with? he wondered as his glance slid to the person beside her. He supposed the man could be called handsome—if you liked that impassive, poker-faced type with cold, blue eyes and a smile that didn't go beyond his lips. Personally, Mike thought he looked as if he'd be as much fun as a trip to the dentist for root-canal surgery. A flash of resentment surged through him at the possessive way the guy had his hand on Ashley's arm.

"There you are, Mike. I've been looking for you," a silky voice purred as Valerie appeared at his side. "Uncle Jack told me to look after you. He'd never forgive me if I allowed you to stand around all by yourself. Let's go get you something to drink, and then we'll find a spot all to ourselves, where we can get better acquainted." She slipped her arm through his.

Still too shaken by the unexpected encounter with Ashley to come up with a way of evading Valerie's attentions, Mike allowed himself to be led away. Glancing back over his shoulder, he had a brief glimpse of Ashley before several other people moved across his line of vision. Gone was the dimple that he'd found so entrancing. Her face looked pale, and the light seemed to have gone out of her eyes.

A huge lump formed in Ashley's throat. For just a second she'd have sworn Mike was delighted to see her. But without warning his expression had turned as hard as granite, leaving her with the feeling that she'd been doused with icy water. And then that—*creature* with the slinky dress and long red fingernails had come along and taken control of him.

No, that wasn't quite fair. After all, Mike was a grown man, capable of making up his own mind. He'd gone with the woman willingly, so he apparently wasn't averse to her attentions. How could he be interested in someone so—so obvious? Ashley wondered. She couldn't help being disappointed in him. Men could be so dense sometimes. . . .

"My dear, how lovely to see you again! So nice that you could come."

Ashley became vaguely aware that someone was speaking to her. With an effort she tore her attention from Mike and his companion and focused on her hostess, who had come to stand by her husband. Stewart's hand was still on her arm, and she felt the pressure of his fingers increasing slightly, as if he were subtly reminding her of her social obligations.

Somehow she managed to find her voice. "Thank you so much for inviting us, Mrs. Sheldon."

"Please call me Lorraine. May I get you a drink? Something to nibble on?"

Ashley must have replied in the affirmative, because she found herself with a glass in one hand, a canapé in the other.

As their hostess's attention was claimed briefly by another guest, Stewart glanced at Ashley and frowned. No doubt he thought she was simply sulking because she hadn't wanted to come to this party. She adjusted her smile, trying to look as if she were enjoying herself as she murmured an appropriate response to something Lorraine was saying.

Wasn't there any way to get out of this woman's clutches? Mike wondered. Valerie had swooped down on him like some predatory bird, just as he was ready to make his break, and now she seemed determined to monopolize him all evening. Somehow she even managed to maneuver him outside through the double doors at the far end of the room. "I want to show you Aunt Lorraine's rose garden," she'd cooed.

He was of an independent nature, and ordinarily he wouldn't allow himself to be coerced into anything against his will, but Valerie's aggressiveness had taken him completely by surprise. He much preferred women who exercised a little more restraint.

Like Ashley Kendall. The thought popped into his mind unbidden.

Once they were outside, it was clear that Valerie had more on her mind than roses. He discovered he had to be fast on his feet to evade her rather obvious advances. She found many reasons to lean close to him, to put her full red lips near his.

"Hadn't we better get back inside?" he suggested when he had just about run out of diversionary tactics. "Your aunt and uncle will be wondering what became of us."

"Oh, they won't worry. They'll know I'm in good hands when I'm with you." Somehow, as she looked up at him through lowered eyelashes, her tone conveyed a double meaning.

By the time he managed to persuade her to go in, he felt as if he'd spent the evening dodging land mines. *This woman sure doesn't give up easily,* he thought.

She turned to him, her lips forming into a pretty pout. "I'd almost think you didn't want to be alone with me," she cooed as she moved closer to him and began toying with his necktie. It was all he could do to keep from brushing her hand away.

* * *

"I always say, the key to financial security is a diversified portfolio," Stewart was intoning to several Flint executives. "Isn't that right, dear?" He glanced at Ashley for confirmation.

"What? Oh—yes, of course." She summoned a bright smile. "I've heard you say that many times."

Would this party never end? she was wondering. She'd hoped she could at least spend the evening circulating among the other guests, but every time she made a move to leave Stewart's side, he'd say something to draw her back into the conversation.

Apparently satisfied that she was still hanging on his every word, Stewart turned his attention back to his audience. Stifling a yawn, Ashley let her glance wander around the room. Although she'd told herself whatever Mike did wasn't of the least concern to her, she couldn't help wondering where he'd disappeared to.

As if her thinking about him had somehow conjured up his presence, he and his blond companion appeared through the double doors at just that moment. The woman drew closer to him and was fingering his tie as she looked up at him in a deliberately seductive manner.

So that was the way it was. Although she couldn't see Mike's expression because his face was in shadow, he didn't seem to be objecting to the woman's attentions. Ashley couldn't suppress a stab of jealousy.

At that moment Mike turned, and Ashley's eyes met his.

Well, two could play that game, she decided. The last thing she wanted was for him to get the idea that it *mattered* to her how many women he'd been out strolling the grounds in the dark with.

When Stewart turned to say something to Ashley just then, she acted instinctively. Linking her arm through his, she smiled up at him in such a way that anyone who happened to be watching would be convinced she was absolutely enamored of him.

She had no way of knowing whether her little charade was having the desired effect on Mike, but it certainly seemed to have worked on Stewart. After an initial second or two of surprise, he looked as if he'd known all along that she would eventually come to her senses.

Uh-oh, now I've done it, Ashley thought, immediately regretting her hasty action. After all the trouble she'd had trying to get through to Stewart that there was nothing between them, she'd probably just undone everything she'd accomplished. Besides, it wasn't fair to him to use him that way. Subterfuge wasn't part of her nature, and she had little respect for women who played one man against another.

The remainder of the evening passed in a kind of daze for Ashley. Before long she felt as if her facial muscles were frozen into a perpetual smile. Afterward she couldn't remember whom she had talked to or what she'd said, but she must have made the proper responses.

Every time she caught sight of Mike, with Valerie clinging to him, something twisted inside her. She might as well admit it, she'd fallen hard for him. And she'd honestly thought her feelings were being reciprocated. But if he preferred someone like that blond man-trap, well, she was better off without him.

So then, why did it hurt so much to see that woman hanging onto him, snuggling up close to him, whispering in his ear as if they had some delicious secret between them?

Thank goodness that's over, Mike thought fervently when he was finally able to elude Valerie and slip away from the party. He wasn't sure which had been worse—spending the evening trying to outmaneuver Valerie, or watching Ashley with that guy—what was his name?—Stewart Lattimer. Something had twisted inside him every time he'd seen Lattimer put his hand on her arm in that possessive way.

He didn't understand how someone like Ashley could be interested in a cold fish like that. She obviously was, though, or she wouldn't have come to the Sheldons' party with him. Well, that just showed how wrong he could be about someone.

He tried to tell himself it was a good thing he'd seen for himself what kind of man appealed to her. The knowledge would go a long way toward putting an end to any foolish romantic notions he might have had.

Somehow that thought didn't make him feel any better, though. All he felt was an acute sense of loss.

Chapter Eleven

As Ashley made her way along Five Mile Drive in Point Defiance Park, occasional glimpses of the Tacoma Narrows were visible through the tall cedars and Douglas firs. Sailboats dotted the sun-dappled blue water, and several small islands, green and misty, could be seen in the distance.

She recalled, with amusement, the invitation that had come in the mail a few days ago. *We've got our act together, and we're taking it on the road*, it had read. Then it went on to say that the Tacoma Players' Junior Theater Arts Class would be making its first public appearance Thursday afternoon at Never Never Land in Point Defiance Park.

She had felt torn. She was reluctant to put herself in a position where she would be likely to run into Mike. Yet she hated to disappoint Brandon. Besides, she had developed a genuine affection for all three of the Shepard children, and she missed seeing them now that school was out.

She steeled herself for the encounter with Mike as she drove past the zoo area of the park and followed the signs that read: NEVER NEVER LAND. If it became necessary to make eye contact with him, she would do so with a brief, impersonal nod, one that would convey the message that she considered him hardly worthy of her notice.

But when she reached the outdoor theater, Mike was nowhere to be seen, although she spotted Sara and Jilly right away. Jilly, clutching the ever-present Woober, waved to get her attention. "Brandon was worried that you wouldn't get here," Sara said as Ashley sat down next to her.

The motherly looking older woman sitting on the other side of the girls leaned across them. "You must be Ashley Kendall. The children talk about you all the time."

"And you're Mrs. Jackson. I'm so glad to meet you."

"I want to thank you for coming to the children's rescue that time the tree fell on my car. I was just frantic, worrying about them. It was such a relief to find out they'd been in good hands."

Ashley resisted the urge to ask where Mike was. She didn't want to give the impression that his whereabouts were of any importance to her. Still, if he had just stepped out for refreshments and was likely to return at any minute, she needed to know that so she could prepare herself. When Jilly solved the problem by confiding, "Uncle Mike couldn't take time off from work today—his job is *very* important, you know," Ashley's relief was tinged with just a touch of disappointment. She told herself it was merely because she wouldn't get the opportunity to show him how little she cared about whether he was there or not.

While they waited for the performance to start, Mrs. Jackson chatted amiably with Ashley. Apparently the housekeeper wasn't aware that Ashley was now persona non grata to Mike, as she mentioned how pleased she was that Ashley was taking such an interest in the children.

The performance consisted of several skits, based—*very* loosely—on old fairy tales, but with a slightly different twist. In one of them Brandon played a knight who had endured a series of rigors so he could slay a dragon and rescue a fair maiden. He was properly nonplussed to find that the damsel had grown tired of waiting and had subdued the dragon herself, made a pet of him, and was giving rides to the village children. Brandon was a natural-born actor, with an innate sense of timing and a flair for comedy. He hammed it up outrageously, and the audience loved it.

After Brandon had been congratulated on a successful acting debut, Mrs. Jackson attempted to gather her little group together. "We still have to stop by the mall and do some shopping," she reminded the children.

Amid groans and eye-rolling from Brandon and resigned expressions from his sisters, the housekeeper explained to Ashley, "I told Mr. Shepard I'd pick up some things for the children. They all need new socks and underwear, and Brandon is due for some new jeans."

"Do we *hafta* go shopping?" Brandon asked.

Mrs. Jackson looked apologetic. "I'm afraid so. Whether we do it now or later, it'll have to be done."

"I know what," Jilly said brightly. "Why don't we

stay here at the park with Ashley while you do your shopping?''

"Now, we can't bother Ashley. I'm sure she has other things to do."

Actually, Ashley didn't, but—the situation with Mike being what it was—she wasn't sure he would appreciate her taking over his children. With three pairs of eyes looking up at her, though, she knew she was outnumbered.

"I'll be glad to take the children," she replied. "We can go over to the zoo. I haven't been there in a long time, and I hear they have a new elephant. It wouldn't be any fun to go by myself, though, so this works out perfectly. Why don't you go ahead and get your shopping done, and I'll bring the children home when we're finished?"

Mrs. Jackson gave in, once she was convinced that Ashley really didn't mind in the least and was, in fact, delighted to have company for the afternoon.

Ashley and the children spent several hours oohing and aahing over the sharks in the aquarium, making the acquaintance of the new elephant, and laughing at the antics of the seals. It was a tired but contented little group that finally made its way back to the parking lot.

As they were leaving the park, Ashley remembered a stop she had to make. "Would you kids mind terribly if we run into a store and pick up some cat food?" she asked. "My cat, Bridget, will be very upset if I come home without it."

All three children, eager to prolong the outing as long as possible, assured her they wouldn't mind a bit.

"Good," Ashley replied, pulling into a small shopping center. "This won't take a minute."

True to her promise, she made her purchase quickly. As they came out of the supermarket, Brandon casually brought it to her attention that there was an ice-cream store on the other side of the parking lot.

"You know, that sounds pretty good," Ashley said. "Let's go get some ice cream." She tossed the cat food into her car, and they set out across the parking lot toward the familiar Baskin-Robbins 31 Flavors sign.

The first distant rumble of thunder sounded just as they reached their destination. Scanning the sky, Ashley saw that a bank of low, threatening clouds was moving in. "It looks as if we might be in for a little rain," she commented as she and the children entered the store.

While they were eating their ice cream, another clap of thunder rang out, so loud they all jumped. Frowning, Ashley glanced out the window. "Maybe we'd better head back to the car while we still can." As they started for the door, she popped the last of her ice-cream cone into her mouth.

But as soon as they stepped outside, big heavy drops of rain began to fall. They picked up momentum until, in a matter of seconds, they became a steady downpour. Ashley's car, on the other side of the parking lot, seemed awfully far away.

As the little group stood under the protective overhang of the roof, watching the rain fall, a familiar silvery-gray BMW suddenly slowed and turned into the parking lot. It glided up next to the ice-cream store and came to a stop. Ashley groaned inwardly as one of the power windows rolled silently down and a voice called out, "Ashley—it *is* you. Lucky I spotted you, since you seem to be stranded. I'm headed for my office right now, but I have a little time to spare. Get in, quick. I'll take you wherever you're headed. We need to talk, anyway."

She knew what Stewart wanted to talk *about*, of course, and she had no desire to rehash what was already firmly settled in her mind. She couldn't imagine why he'd want to plead his case with three children in the backseat taking it all in, anyway. "Thanks," she called back, "but I have my car here. It's just across the parking lot."

"I'll take you there, then." He leaned across the seat to open the door for her.

"No, Stewart, really—"

Her words were interrupted as a horn tooted impatiently behind Stewart's car. "Now, Ashley, don't be stubborn," he said. "I can't sit here blocking traffic."

The horn sounded again. Stewart frowned, but Ashley wasn't sure if it was meant for her—because she was being "stubborn"—or for the impatient driver behind him.

"But St—"

"Just get in, please."

"Oh, all right," she replied with a sigh. If she didn't, there was no telling how long he'd sit there tying up traffic. "Come on, kids," she called. Leaving the protection of the overhang, they made a dash for Stewart's car. As the three children scrambled into the backseat, she said, "Stewart, these are my friends,

Sara, Brandon, and Jilly. Oh, and Woober. Kids, I'd like you to meet Stewart Lattimer.''

The expression that came over Stewart's face was one of stunned horror. He paled visibly, and his mouth opened and closed several times, like a fish gasping for air. At first Ashley thought wildly that he must be choking or having a heart attack. But then the reason for his odd behavior dawned on her. Apparently it hadn't occurred to him that these children were with *her*. He must have thought they just happened to be standing there waiting for the rain to stop, just as she was.

Knowing Stewart as she did, she should have realized, of course, that the last thing he'd want in his new car would be three children eating ice-cream cones. But it had been hard to think clearly, with him snapping orders at her and that other driving honking his horn.

''My car is over by the supermarket,'' she pointed out gently. Muttering something under his breath, Stewart shifted into gear and started off jerkily.

As they made the short trip across the parking lot, Jilly ran sticky fingers across the soft plush of the upholstery with a sort of awed fascination while Brandon played with the power windows. When Sara admonished him, under her breath, ''Don't handle things,'' he abandoned that form of diversion and leaned over Stewart's shoulder to examine the dash. ''Hey, Mr. Lattimer, what does that button do?'' he asked, pointing.

''Brandon, be caref—'' Ashley began as she noticed that his ice cream was dripping over the edge of the cone. But it was too late. While she watched helplessly, a glob of fudge royale trickled down onto Stewart's lapel. His expression was unreadable as he took a spotless white handkerchief from his breast pocket and scrubbed ineffectually at the ice cream.

By the time they reached their destination, Stewart was tight-lipped, and there was a noticeable twitch on one side of his face. "I must say, Ashley," he began as they pulled up next to her car, "you might have told me. . . ."

She refrained from pointing out that he hadn't given her a chance. "Thank you so much." She smiled her sweetest smile. "We certainly appreciate your giving us a lift. Don't we, children?" she prompted as they got out of the car.

"Yes, thank you," they chorused dutifully, and Brandon added, "Neat car, Mr. Lattimer."

Stewart muttered something unintelligible—it sounded as if he were strangling—and sped off in a squeal of tires.

"He's kind of nervous, isn't he?" Brandon observed.

Serves him right for being so bossy, Ashley thought as she watched his car disappear into traffic. He had looked as if he were going to faint when the children had climbed into his car with their ice-cream cones. It occurred to her that he was probably thoroughly convinced she'd engineered the whole thing just to annoy him.

By the time Ashley delivered her young charges back home, the rain had stopped and the clouds were starting to dissipate. The children had so much to tell Mrs. Jackson, their words tumbled over each other.

"We saw elephants and polar bears and—"

"And then we had some ice cream—"

"And when we came out of the ice-cream store, it was raining, and the car was 'way over on the other side of the parking lot, but Ashley's friend came along and gave us a ride to her car—"

The account was interrupted by a cry of dismay from Jilly. All eyes turned toward the little girl.

"I left Woober in that man's car."

Ashley's heart sank. The idea of facing Stewart again—especially before he'd had time to recover from his anger—made her feel as if a heavy rock had lodged itself in the pit of her stomach. Maybe in a few days. . . .

She knelt down so that she was at eye level with Jilly. "Honey, I don't know when I'll be seeing Mr. Lattimer again, but I'm sure Woober will be fine in the backseat of his car for a little while."

Silently Jilly shook her head.

"It's a very comfortable car," Ashley added hopefully.

Jilly's lower lip quivered, and her eyes filled with tears. "No, I have to have him back right away," she wailed. "He'll be lonesome without me."

Over Jilly's head Ashley exchanged glances with Mrs. Jackson, but the housekeeper looked as helpless as Ashley felt. Ashley recalled Mike's words: *". . . hardly ever lets Woober out of her sight . . ."* and *". . . she clung to that teddy bear as if it represented the only security in the world. . . ."*

It looked as if there were no way around it. "I'll go right over and get Woober for you," she promised.

Jilly's heartfelt, "Oh, thank you," was accompanied by a tearful smile.

Ashley located Stewart's car in the parking lot of his office building. Peeking in the back window, she could see Woober reclining against the plush seat. She tried the doors, just on the off chance that Stewart had forgotten to lock them, but, of course, he was never careless about such matters.

She found his outer office empty. There went her last hope—that she could have his secretary get the key for her. She could hear low, businesslike voices coming from the inner office. Gathering her courage, she rapped gently on the door. The voices broke off and, after a pause, Stewart called out, "Yes?"

"Stewart, it's Ashley. I have to talk to you."

"Can't it wait? I'm in the middle of a business meeting."

"No, it can't. This is important."

After another brief pause, the door opened and Stewart stood glaring at her. Ashley winced slightly at the dried stain on his lapel. Behind him the two men he'd been conferring with suspended their conversation while they waited for him to take care of the interruption.

"Well?" he asked, his face like a thundercloud.

She had intended to state her business in a calm, levelheaded manner, but at the sight of his stern expression she promptly forgot her carefully rehearsed little speech. "Jilly left Woober in the backseat of your car, and I need to get him back," she blurted out. "If you'll let me borrow your key, I'll take care of it myself, and you can get on with your meeting.''

One of the men behind Stewart raised his eyebrows in surprise, and the other looked somewhat alarmed.

Ashley leaned a little to one side, so she could see past Stewart. ''Woober is a teddy bear,'' she explained to the two men. She could feel her cheeks reddening. ''Actually, his name is J. Worthington Bear, but Jilly couldn't say that when she was little. . . .'' Her voice trailed off as she realized she was babbling. ''He—he means a lot to Jilly. She's only six, you see . . .'' she finished up lamely. She noticed one of the men's lips twitching in amusement.

Stewart rolled his eyes heavenward. ''You interrupted my meeting for a *teddy bear*?''

Ashley suppressed a flash of anger. ''I promised Jilly I'd get it back,'' she said, regaining some of her composure.

With the air of one whose patience was being sorely tried, Stewart dug into his pocket and handed her a set of keys. Then, turning back to the two men, he said, ''Now then, gentlemen, where were we?''

Ashley rushed down to the parking lot and retrieved Woober. When she came back upstairs to return the keys, Stewart accepted them wordlessly.

Am I glad that's over, she thought with a profound sigh of relief as she headed back to Mike's to return the teddy bear to its rightful owner.

Before long her normally good spirits began to assert themselves. True, she had embarrassed herself by bursting wild-eyed into Stewart's meeting with a frantic tale of Woober being locked in his car, but the scene hadn't been without its more amusing aspects—such as the astonished expressions on the faces of those other two men.

Besides, the whole episode might have been a blessing in disguise. Now that she'd committed the unpardonable sin of making an utter fool of herself in front of Stewart's business associates, maybe he'd finally accept the fact that she wasn't the woman for him.

Brandon had been understanding about Mike's not being able to come to his opening performance. "I know you can't just take a day off from work any old time," he'd said. "Especially when you're right in the middle of a project." Still, Mike couldn't help feeling he *should* have been there. It crossed his mind, as he maneuvered his car through the late-afternoon traffic, that there was more to this business of being a father than just providing food and shelter.

All day at the plant his thoughts had been more on what was happening out at Point Defiance Park than on the servo-control system he was redesigning. Didn't he owe it to Brandon to be on hand to cheer him on— or to offer sympathy if it was needed? What if the kid forgot his lines, or his mustache wouldn't stick to his upper lip, or— or he fell off the stage?

Besides, now that Brandon had found something he was really interested in—besides getting into mischief—he was entitled to all the support he could get. Enrolling him in that theater-arts class had been a stroke of genius. Not that Mike deserved any of the credit, he reminded himself with a twinge of guilt. He would never had thought of it on his own. The whole thing had been strictly Ashley's idea.

And how had he repaid her? a little voice inside him asked. In his mind he replayed that scene in Applegate's office, when he'd gotten all hostile and defensive because he'd thought she was making an accusation against Brandon.

Ever since the incident, his conscience had been giving him little nudges, which he'd stubbornly ignored. Now it gave him the mental equivalent of a good swift kick in the pants. He cringed at the memory of how insufferably self-righteous he must have sounded. He knew he had a tendency to overreact where the kids were concerned, but he should have realized Ashley had never had anything but Brandon's best interests at heart.

He wondered what it would take to get back into her good graces. Maybe if he called her and admitted he'd acted like a complete idiot and threw himself on her mercy, she might take pity on him and give him a second chance. It was worth a try, anyway.

But then he remembered that guy she'd been with at the Sheldons' party. What was his name? They'd been introduced sometime during the evening. Stewart something. Stewart Lattimer. He wondered how involved she was with him. But surely he could beat old Stew's time, he thought. By the time he pulled into his garage, he'd convinced himself that he had a fairly good chance of squaring things with Ashley.

"How did the performance go?" he asked as he entered the house.

"It was great!" Brandon replied. "And I was terrific."

Mrs. Jackson glanced in from the kitchen, where she was putting the finishing touches on dinner before taking her leave. "You would have been proud of him."

"He *was* pretty good," Sara put in.

" 'Pretty good!' " Brandon echoed. "I had the audience eating out of my hand."

Mike smiled indulgently. Modesty wasn't one of Brandon's strongest points. "I suppose we can expect the offers from Hollywood to start rolling in any day."

Amid the lighthearted banter, one voice was noticeably silent. Jilly, sitting on the couch, wasn't joining in. Her large, usually lively eyes had lost their animation, and there was a woebegone expression on her face.

Mike sat down beside her and took her on his lap. "Hey, what's wrong?" he asked gently.

"It's Woober. He's lost."

"Lost, huh? Maybe he's just hiding, to play a trick on you. I'll bet if we look around, we can find that old bear."

Jilly shook her head. "He's not here. He got left in the car after Ashley took us for ice cream. She had to go back and get him."

"Ashley?" Mike repeated, bewildered.

"After we went to the zoo and the 'quarium—" the little girl started to explain. All at once her face lighted up as she saw something out the window. "Here she is now! And she's got Woober." She squirmed down from his lap and ran to the door.

Mike felt a sudden leap of excitement as, following Jilly's glance, he saw that Ashley was at this moment getting out of her car in his driveway, carrying the worn brown teddy bear. His first impulse was to rush out to meet her with the same carefree abandon as Jilly, but he forced himself to use a little restraint. He didn't want to overwhelm her.

"Now what's this about the zoo and the aquarium and ice cream?" he asked Sara and Brandon as they accompanied him to the door.

"Ashley came to see our performance," Brandon explained. "I sent her an invitation. Anyway, after it was over, we didn't want to go shopping with Mrs. Jackson, so Ashley said, why didn't we go to the zoo with her. And then after she bought cat food for Bridget, we went for ice cream—"

They were outside now. Mike hesitated on the top step, suddenly unsure of himself. Jilly was unhampered by any such reservations, however, and threw herself against Ashley with enthusiasm.

As Ashley bent down to return the hug, she looked up and her eyes met Mike's over the little girl's head. Several charged heartbeats of time thudded between her and Mike as their glances locked. Her smile was tentative, but it was enough to bring that dimple into play.

She looked so lovely—so altogether appealing—that Mike's heart contracted. He wanted to rush to her and take her in his arms, to tell her he loved her—for it suddenly occurred to him, with startling clarity, that he *was* in love with her—and to beg her forgiveness for having behaved like such a stupid jerk. The only thing that restrained him was the thought that he didn't want his declaration of love to take place in full view of the entire neighborhood, not to mention his children.

Taking a deep, ragged breath, he struggled to bring his emotions under control. *Slow and easy, old man,* he told himself as he started down the steps, with Sara and Brandon on either side of him. "So, after you got your ice cream, Jilly left Woober in Ashley's car?" he asked them, in an attempt to restore normalcy to the situation.

"No, she left him in that other car," Sara explained. "Ashley's friend, Mr. Lattimer, gave us a ride, and that's when Woober got left behind—"

"Mr. Lattimer?" The words came out so sharply that both children looked at him in surprise.

"Stewart Lattimer." Brandon took up the thread of the story. "He's got this real neat car—"

Mike was almost at the bottom of the steps now, face-to-face with Ashley. As Brandon's words sank in, a shock wave of pain ran through him and settled like a rock in his midsection. The pleasure he'd felt a few seconds earlier faded away like a wisp of smoke.

So she'd taken the kids along—*his* kids—while she'd been out with that Lattimer character this afternoon. The thought made him burn with anger. Maybe if she'd been paying more attention to the kids and less to good old Stewart, Woober wouldn't have gotten left behind.

An icy knot of apprehension formed inside Ashley as she noted Mike's sudden change of expression. Watching him descend the steps, she'd been certain he was pleased to see her. It had been evident in his eyes, in his bearing, in the frail little tendrils of feeling that had started to weave their way between them. He'd been talking to Sara and Brandon as he came downstairs, and, at something one of them had said, his face had suddenly become a stony mask of aloofness.

"I—ah—I brought Woober back to Jilly," she said in faltering tones.

"I see that. I hope it wasn't too much trouble." His tone was frigid.

"No. No trouble at all." She turned her attention back to Jilly so he wouldn't see the watery fullness that had sprung to her eyes. "Woober didn't seem to mind at all that he got left behind. I think he rather enjoyed his little adventure, but I'm sure he's glad to be back home." Giving the little girl a final hug, she started back to her car.

She hoped Mike would call her name, would ask her not to leave. Instead, he stood by silently as she got in and started backing out of the driveway, blinking back the shimmering tears that blurred her vision. She carefully avoided looking in his direction. Although she was seething inwardly with a chaotic mixture of hurt and controlled anger, she would have faced a firing squad rather than allow him to see her pain.

Chapter Twelve

"Ashley, I really, really, *really* need you to do something for me." Sara's voice over the phone was earnest and persuasive.

"Maybe you'd better tell me what it is, first," Ashley replied cautiously.

"My Girl Scout troop is having a mother-daughter dinner Thursday evening, and I—I need someone to go with me."

At the wistful note in Sara's tone, Ashley's heart went out to her. But as much as she wanted to grant the child's request, she had a feeling to do so would be inviting trouble. The way things stood between her and Mike right now, he would probably suspect her of having some ulterior motive.

"Have you thought about asking Mrs. Jackson?" she suggested. "I'm sure she'd be glad to go with you?"

"But I'd rather have *you*. Besides, Mrs. Jackson can't go because she'll be taking care of Brandon and Jilly. Uncle Mike had to go to California again and won't be back until Friday morning. Mrs. Jackson is staying with us while he's gone."

"Did you talk this over with your uncle before he left?" She wondered whose idea it had been for Sara to ask Ashley to accompany her.

There was a long pause before Sara replied, "No, I didn't mention the dinner to him at all. I just wasn't planning to go, since it's for mothers and daughters. . . ." Her voice trailed off, but what she *didn't* say wrung Ashley's heart. "But then I thought of asking you," she went on.

Ashley made a quick decision. "I'd love to go with you." If Mike didn't like it, that was just too bad. Right now she was more concerned with Sara's feelings than with his.

"Oh, Mr. Shepard, we weren't expecting you back from California until tomorrow," Mrs. Jackson said when Mike let himself in the front door.

"I finished up early, so I decided to come home tonight instead of hanging around until morning." He glanced around. "Where is everybody?"

"Jilly and Brandon are in the den, and Sara's Girl Scout troop is having a mother-daughter dinner. She should be getting home any minute now."

At the words *mother-daughter dinner,* Mike felt a stab of pain. His imagination conjured up a picture of the child tagging wistfully along with one of her friends and the friend's mother, like a piece of extra luggage. "She didn't say anything to me about a mother-daughter dinner," he said, frowning. "Who'd she go with?"

"That nice Ashley Kendall took her. I'd have been

glad to go myself, but I had to stay here and look after the other children, of course.''

Mike felt a rush of gratitude toward Ashley for stepping in and helping his niece out of what could have been an uncomfortable situation.

And she'd be coming here in a little while to bring Sara home! This could be the opportunity he'd been hoping for—if he didn't blow it by pulling another of those really stupid stunts, that seemed to characterize his every move lately.

For the past couple of weeks— ever since the kids had explained what they'd been doing in Stewart Lattimer's car—he'd been berating himself for being so thickheaded. Apparently the guy had merely given them a lift across the parking lot in the rain. And, according to the kids' account of what had taken place, Ashley had seemed annoyed that he'd shown up at all. But at the mention of Stewart Lattimer, Mike had jumped to a wrong conclusion instead of taking time to find out the whole story.

A dozen times since then he'd been tempted to call Ashley and try to apologize for his boorish behavior. But every time he reached for the phone, he lost his nerve at the last minute. More than likely, she'd slam the phone down at the sound of his voice. Not that he'd blame her.

This wasn't the sort of thing that could be handled over the phone, anyway, he told himself. If there were any chance that something could be salvaged out of the mess he'd made, he needed to talk to her in person. Now, if he could just get the kids to give them a little privacy. . . .

* * *

Ashley was feeling pleasantly relaxed and mellow as she and Sara approached the Shepard house. All the way home they'd been teasing each other and joking as if they were the same age.

Any misgivings she'd had about whether she might have overstepped her bounds had been dispelled once they'd arrived at the dinner. There was nothing like spending the evening in the company of a group of lively ten-year-olds to help put one's priorities in the proper order, she reflected—the camaraderie among the girls in the troop, the lighthearted banter, not to mention the warm rapport that was growing between herself and Sara. . . .

"Look, Uncle Mike's home!" Sara exclaimed, breaking into her thoughts.

Ashley's buoyant mood evaporated at the sight of the blue sedan in the driveway. "I thought you said he wasn't due back until tomorrow."

"That's what he told us," Sara replied. "He must have changed his plans."

As soon as Ashley pulled into the driveway, the front door opened, and she could see Mike's tall frame silhouetted in the entry hall. Because of the way the light was shining behind him, she couldn't make out his expression as he descended the steps, but determination was evident in his every movement.

Whatever he had on his mind, she simply wasn't in the mood, she decided. She'd had enough of his high-handedness, his arrogance, and his disapproving frowns. If it bothered him that she'd stepped in when Sara needed her—well, that was *his* problem, not hers, and she certainly wasn't going to apologize for her actions. She didn't intend to speak to him at all if she could avoid it. She rolled her window down so she could say a quick good-bye to Sara and be on her way.

Sara was out of the car as soon as it stopped, leaving the door hanging open. "Uncle Mike, I'm so glad you're back!" she cried, giving him a hug. "Look who's with me."

As Mike returned her embrace, he said under his breath, "Why don't you let me talk to Ashley in private for a few minutes?"

Sara's eyes widened as she glanced over her shoulder at Ashley and then looked back at Mike again. She nodded, a little conspiratorial smile playing around her mouth. *Something* was obviously going on between her two favorite people, and she was more than willing to make herself scarce if it would help the situation along. With a hurried, " 'Night, Ashley—thanks for going with me," she rushed up the steps.

What had he said to Sara to make her disappear like that? Ashley wondered as she leaned across the seat to pull the passenger door closed. When she straightened up again, she gave a little gasp of surprise as she found herself gazing directly into Mike's eyes. He had come around to her side of the car and was standing there with his arms resting on the bottom of the open window.

All at once her pulse seemed to be pounding at an alarming rate, and she was having trouble catching her breath. *It's just because he startled me,* she told herself, relieved that the darkness hid the sudden color that rushed to her face. Whatever he wanted, she hoped he would just speak his piece and then move back out of the way so she could leave—before he sensed the effect his closeness was having on her.

She couldn't see his expression because his face was in shadow, but his tone was low and gentle as he said, "I really appreciate your taking Sara to that dinner."

This wasn't what she was expecting, and she was caught off guard. "I—I'm glad I was able to help," she murmured, making an effort to control the shakiness in her voice.

"Ah—listen, Ashley—if I can get Mrs. Jackson to stay with the kids for a while longer, do you suppose we could go someplace and—and talk?"

She shot him a wary look as memories of their last meeting flashed through her mind. What was he up to now? she wondered. Whatever it was, she had no intention of allowing him to hurt her again. Swallowing hard, she forced herself to meet his gaze. "I don't think we have anything to say to each other," she said coldly, echoing his own words to her of a few weeks ago.

Mike recoiled as if he'd been struck. For a second or two Ashley regretted her harsh words, but she hardened her emotions. *How does it feel when the shoe is on the other foot?* she wanted to ask. She felt no thrill of triumph, however, only a dull emptiness.

As he stepped away from the car, she quickly shifted into reverse and started backing out of the driveway, ignoring Mike's, "Ashley, wait—"

Just before she drove off, she caught a slight movement at the living-room window, as if a curtain were being pulled aside. Glancing up, she spotted three faces watching the proceedings with wide-eyed interest. Just then a taller figure appeared behind them—that would be Mrs. Jackson, of course. The housekeeper must have told the children not to stare at her and Mike, because the curtain fell back into place, but not before Ashley had time to notice three identical expressions of disappointment.

Mike lay awake most of the night, staring into the darkness. Every time he closed his eyes, he saw Ashley pulling out of his driveway as if she couldn't get away from him fast enough. And with that memory came a quick stab of pain.

Sometime in the early hours of the morning he finally admitted the truth—that he was so totally, irrevocably in love with Ashley that a future without her seemed bleak and empty beyond belief. It did no good to try to tell himself that he had no room in his life for romantic entanglements or that she was already involved with someone else, anyway. There it was. He loved Ashley Kendall, and nothing in the world was going to change that.

Having come to terms with that fact, his logical engineer's mind asked, *Well, what do you intend to do about it?*

After mulling over his options, he realized his only possible course of action was to go to her, admit his mistakes, and do whatever was necessary to get back into her good graces.

Not that he had any right to expect her to listen to him, after the way he'd behaved, but *somehow* he'd find a way to make her understand how sorry he was.

She *had* to believe him and forgive him. Anything else just didn't bear thinking about. He made up his mind he'd go and talk to her as soon as possible, before he lost his nerve.

Saturday afternoon would be the best time to do it, he decided, while the kids were all busy with their own pursuits. Sara's Girl Scout troop was going roller-skating, Jilly had been invited to a birthday party, and Brandon was going to the movies with a friend. For a few hours, at least, his time would be his own.

He was feeling more optimistic as he dropped off to sleep. Everything was going to work out fine.

"Don't forget, Uncle Mike, you have to take Dawg in for his bath this afternoon," Sara reminded him Saturday morning, glancing at the calendar.

He *had* forgotten. After that fiasco when Brandon had tried to give the dog a bath, Mike had decided life would be much simpler if the job were turned over to professionals. Dawg had a standing appointment, the first Saturday of every month, to be bathed and de-fleaed. But dropping him off at the grooming parlor would involve only a slight revision of plans, Mike realized. He had to go right by there on his way to Ashley's.

But when he walked into The Classy Pet with Dawg, the young woman who owned the shop seemed surprised to see him. "Didn't anybody call you?" she asked, dismayed. "Someone was supposed to let you know we can't take Dawg today—but I guess nobody got around to it. It's been a madhouse around here. Two of my employees didn't show up, and we're running 'way behind. I'd work Dawg in if there were any way at all, but it takes longer to do a dog that size. And sometimes he's a little—well, rambunctious.'' She gave him an apologetic smile.

Mike's thoughts raced ahead. If he took Dawg back home now, that wouldn't leave him much time to plead his case with Ashley before all the kids got back from their various activities. He'd just have to take the animal along with him and leave him in the car while he talked to Ashley. He'd park in the shade, leave the windows open, and hope for the best. Brandon had been taking Dawg to obedience classes for several weeks, and Mike recalled that *Stay* had been one of the first commands taught in the class. By now the dog ought to have developed at least a rudimentary idea of what was expected of him.

Well, so much for best-laid plans, he thought as he pulled away from The Classy Pet with a grinning Dawg in the backseat, head hanging out the window and ears flapping in the breeze. When he'd made up his mind to go to Ashley and get things settled without further delay, he hadn't counted on taking along a large, over-active dog.

When he arrived at Ashley's apartment building, Mike noted that her car was in its accustomed place. *So far, so good,* he thought as he pulled into a shady spot next to a new-looking BMW. At least *something* was going according to plan.

''Stay,'' he commanded to Dawg in his most authoritative voice. He was feeling confident as he started across the parking lot. He had a feeling things were going to go well this time.

*   *   *

Ashley puttered around her apartment all morning, unable to keep her mind on any one project. By noontime she finally gave up all hope of getting anything constructive accomplished. Changing into a brief two-piece bathing suit, she grabbed a book and her suntan lotion and went out to sit in a lounge chair by the apartment swimming pool.

She tossed her romance novel aside impatiently when she realized she'd read the same page three times, and it had made no more sense than if it had been written in Sanskrit. With a sigh, she tilted her head back and closed her eyes.

Her thoughts kept going back to that encounter with Mike the other night and the hurt expression in his eyes when she'd told him they had nothing to say to each other. Telling herself he deserved it did nothing to ease the knot of emptiness inside her. Did she really want it to end this way? She could always say she still had her pride, but pride was a cold substitute for what she knew she and Mike could have—if they could just get together long enough to settle their differences. How had everything gotten so complicated?

She frowned slightly as a shadow fell across her face, blocking out the sun. When she'd come out here, the pool area had been deserted. She hoped one of her neighbors wasn't going to be in the mood for conversation. Glancing up through half-closed eyes, she stifled a groan at the sight of Stewart looking down at her. She thought of pretending to be asleep, but it was too late. He'd already seen her eyelids flutter.

"Stewart, what are you doing here?" she asked,

getting up. She hadn't seen him since the teddy bear incident, and she'd begun to hope he'd finally given up on her. Was he going to keep turning up forever, like a bad penny?

"I knew you had to be home because I saw your car in the parking lot. When you didn't answer, I thought you might be out here."

"What was it you wanted to see me about?" she asked in the politely impersonal tone she usually reserved for dealing with telephone solicitors.

Stewart's eyes narrowed. "I must say, that's not a very cordial welcome—"

Ashley bit back a sharp reply. She just wanted him to state his business and leave. "You were saying?" she prompted.

"Oh—yes. I came over because I thought it's about time we got things settled between us."

"Things?" Ashley echoed warily. "What 'things'?"

"Don't pretend you don't know what I'm talking about. I'm a patient man, but this foolishness has been going on long enough."

Ashley didn't bother to suppress a sigh of exasperation. What was it going to take to get through to him that she wasn't simply playing hard to get?

But before she could frame an appropriately scathing reply, her attention was diverted by someone approaching across the courtyard. A sharp tingle of excitement, mixed with apprehension, shot through her as she recognized Mike's tall figure. Was she imagining things? she wondered, bewildered. Maybe she'd had too much sun. But no, he was very real—so real she could see the wisps of dark hair that curled against the V of his open sport shirt, and the gleam of determination in his eyes. Even in her confused state, she couldn't help noticing the way his well-fitting jeans emphasized the whipcord leanness of his body, of how the faded denim molded his trim hips and thighs. The thought brought a splash of color to her cheeks.

As he came toward her with purposeful strides, he had the air of a person who had a mission to fulfill and didn't intend to be deterred from it. "Ashley, I have to talk to you," he said, his voice low and earnest.

Stewart moved closer to her and reached out as if to put a possessive hand on her arm. Almost instinctively she stepped out of his way. The gesture wasn't lost on either man. Stewart made no attempt to suppress a resentful frown, while Mike's expression indicated approval of her action.

What do I do now? Ashley wondered as her two visitors stood glaring at each other, like gladiators preparing to do battle. Everything was happening too fast. She felt as if she'd blundered into someone else's dream and didn't know her lines.

Mike turned his attention back to Ashley, as if Stewart were hardly worthy of notice. "We really need to talk."

"Ah—excuse me," Stewart put in stiffly, "but Ashley and I were in the middle of a conversation."

Mike ignored him as if he hadn't spoken. Somehow he managed to put himself between Ashley and Stewart. As he moved closer to her, the scent of his after-shave teased her senses and turned her insides to jelly.

"Please hear me out—"

"Ashley, now really—" Stewart interrupted.

"Is there someplace we can talk in private?" There was no mistaking Mike's meaning as he glanced briefly over his shoulder at Stewart. He put his hands on her upper arms, and she had to stifle a little involuntary gasp at the sensations the light touch generated on her bare skin. "This is important."

Something in his tone caused her to search his face. The look she saw there caused a tiny explosion deep inside her. She sensed that whatever he wanted to say to her, this could be the most important conversation of her life. After a moment of hesitation, barely as long as a heartbeat, she gave an almost imperceptible nod, hardly taking her eyes from his. . . .

"Ashley—" Stewart's irritated voice sliced through the web of feeling that was drawing them together.

During that brief distraction, Mike's attention was drawn to a point just behind Ashley. At his muffled exclamation, she glanced around just in time to see Dawg loping across the courtyard toward them, his mouth open and his tongue lolling out in a grin of welcome.

Looking back on the incident later, Ashley was never quite sure just what happened in the next few seconds. Everything took place so fast, the events were sort of blurred together in her mind. She did remember Bridget, who had chosen that moment to stroll across the courtyard, giving a little warning growl as she spotted the approaching dog.

At this new diversion, Dawg's ears lifted in interest. Then all at once Bridget's small body was an orange streak hurtling toward the pool area, followed closely by Dawg's lumbering form. Mike, recognizing the potential for disaster, dropped his hands from Ashley's arms and made a grab for the dog as he sped past, but the animal eluded his grasp.

When Bridget leaped across the corner of the pool, some vestige of good sense warned Dawg that attempting a similar feat would be unwise. His massive body wasn't built for maneuverability, though, and his huge paws slipped clumsily on the wet tile as he tried to change course.

"What the—" Stewart exclaimed just before Dawg careened into him.

Ashley watched in horrified fascination as Stewart teetered precariously on the edge of the pool, for what seemed an eternity, before losing his balance. He seemed to be moving in slow motion, his arms flailing as if trying to grab onto the air, as he toppled into the water. In the meantime Bridget scampered up the nearest tree, where she perched on one of the lower branches and made vicious swipes with her paw at the furiously barking dog. Ashley and Mike both rushed to the side of the pool as Stewart stood up, waist deep in water. Even dripping wet, he'd lost none of his poise. In fact, he seemed even more coolly dignified than usual, his face a study in controlled anger. Ignoring Mike's extended hand, he sloshed over to the ladder and climbed out.

Ashley tried to look properly concerned, but she was having trouble keeping a straight face. Stewart did look awfully silly, standing there dripping wet, with his hair hanging down around his face like limp seaweed. She knew she ought to say *something*, but she was afraid if she opened her mouth at all, she wouldn't be able to contain the gales of laughter that threatened to overwhelm her.

"Look, I'm really sorry about this," Mike apologized, both to Ashley and to Stewart. "I told Dawg to stay in the car—" He broke off as Ashley gave a little choking sound. "Are you all right?" he asked, concerned.

She nodded, keeping her lips pressed together tightly.

"That animal," Stewart ground out, biting off the words, "should be put away. He's a menace."

Mike's glance held Ashley's for a fraction of a second. "I'd better go," he said under his breath, as if he sensed that his presence was only making things worse. Without another word he grabbed Dawg's collar and started toward the parking lot.

Ashley felt a pang of emptiness as she watched him leave. She longed to call him back, but the laughter she'd been struggling to hold back had been replaced by a huge lump in her throat.

Once he was out of sight, she drew a deep sigh and turned back to Stewart. She supposed she owed him at least common courtesy. "Is there—is there anything I can do?" she asked when she finally had her voice under control. "Let me get you a towel—"

He glared at her. "I just want to get away from this madhouse." He turned and strode away, squishing with every step. Watching him go, Ashley gave a little shrug.

*   *   *

"Boy, we really blew that, didn't we?" Mike said to Dawg as he pulled out of the parking lot. "We'll be lucky if she ever speaks to us again. Never mind trying to get back into my good graces," he muttered when Dawg planted two large paws on the back of the driver's seat and rested his chin on Mike's shoulder. "I'm mad at you."

But when he glanced into the rearview mirror, he caught a glimpse of the expression in the soulful brown eyes. "Okay, I forgive you," he said with a resigned sigh. He reached back to pat the shaggy head. "At least we gave old Stew something to remember us by."

Chapter Thirteen

"**I** don't think I ever actually grasped the true meaning of the phrase 'mixed emotions' until today," Ashley said, taking Bridget onto her lap. "I can't say I was sorry to see Stewart dumped into the pool. I mean, it wasn't as if he'd been in danger, or anything like that. He fell into the shallow end. And maybe he's finally out of my hair once and for all. It didn't do any good to tell him I didn't want to see him anymore—he just refused to accept that—but I think the insult to his dignity may have done the trick."

Bridget lifted her head to have her chin scratched.

"But, on the other hand," Ashley went on as she obliged, "it looks as if we might have scared Mike away too. He took off in such a hurry yesterday, he probably thinks I blame him for what happened to Stewart."

She gave a resigned shrug. Between *his* children and dog and *her* cat, it appeared that whatever might have been between herself and Mike had been effectively nipped in the bud, almost before it had gotten started. It was probably just as well, she told herself, since it seemed that all they did was hurt each other.

That thought only made her feel worse. Suddenly she had a dismal vision of the rest of her life stretching out ahead of her without Mike in it. She pictured a series of long, dreary evenings spent sharing her innermost feelings with her cat. This prospect was so depressing that she felt her eyes beginning to mist over.

Bridget rubbed the top of her head against Ashley's chin, as if in sympathy. ''It's nothing against you,'' Ashley murmured as she caressed the silky head.

She was working up to a good case of self-pity when the doorbell rang. She wiped the back of her hand across her eyes before putting Bridget off her lap and getting up to answer it.

A little gasp of astonishment escaped her lips when she opened the door and found Brandon and Dawg on her doorstep. She was quite sure she'd never seen a more pathetic sight in her life. Brandon's thin shoulders were slumped, and every particle of his being conveyed an attitude of utter dejection. His face was dirty, and his T-shirt was half in and half out of his jeans. A bulky backpack hung over one shoulder, and in his hand he grasped a frayed rope, the other end of which was tied to Dawg's collar. Even the dog seemed uncharacteristically subdued, his ears and tail both drooping dispiritedly.

As Ashley stared down at the pair, speechless, Brandon drew a deep, quavery sigh, as if he were making a manly effort to hold back tears. It was obvious he had already been crying. His eyes were red, and there were little rivulets running down his face, through the dirt.

All thoughts of Ashley's own troubles vanished.

"Brandon, what are you doing here?" she exclaimed when she managed to find her voice. "How did you get here?" The Shepard house was several miles from her apartment.

"We walked over. We're running away."

"I see," Ashley replied, a multitude of thoughts running through her mind. Her conscience told her it was her duty to call Mike right away—he must be frantic with worry—but she felt she owed it to Brandon to find out what was going on first. Whether his problem was real or imagined, he was obviously a very troubled child right now, and he'd come to her for help. Putting a hand on his shoulder, she drew him inside gently.

As Dawg followed Brandon into the apartment, Bridget arched her back and emitted a menacing hiss. "Oh, hush," Ashley ordered impatiently. "Is that any way to behave?" She had more urgent matters to cope with right now than soothing a cat whose feelings were ruffled because she felt her territory was being violated.

When they were in the living room, Brandon turned to Ashley. "Can me'n Dawg live with you?"

"Well, that's something we'll have to discuss. Running away from home is a pretty big step, you know. I suppose you're thought this over carefully."

"Uh-huh. We can't stay there anymore." There was a wistful note in his voice. "We have to find another place to live."

"And why is that? Aren't you happy at home?" What had gone on at his house, she wondered, to upset him so badly that he felt he had no choice but to run away?

There was a long, meaningful pause before Brandon burst out with, "Uncle Mike says I have to get rid of Dawg!"

Ashley was barely able to hold back an exclamation of astonishment and anger. Surely Mike must know how much that dog meant to the boy. But maybe Brandon had misunderstood. "Are you *sure* that's what he said?" she asked.

Brandon nodded his head earnestly. "He said we're going to have to 'do something' about Dawg. I saw a program on television where this kid's dad said the same thing, and then he took their dog to the pound. And you know what happens to dogs there—"

At the despair in his voice, Ashley's heart went out to him. She held out her arms and Brandon came into them, sobbing as if his heart were breaking. As she soothed the distraught child, she was thinking, *How could Mike even consider such a thing?* Didn't he realize how traumatic it would be for Brandon to have to give up his beloved pet, after losing both parents? She could hardly believe she'd been so wrong in her judgment of him. She'd honestly thought he had the children's best interests at heart in spite of his inexperience, but if he could do something like this, he didn't deserve to be a parent.

"Don't worry, I won't let anyone send Dawg to the pound," she reassured Brandon when he finally seemed all cried out.

"B-but Uncle Mike said—" Brandon began.

"We'll just see about this," Ashley said, going to the phone and punching out the number of the Shepard house. She'd let Mr. Mike Shepard know exactly what she thought of a man who could be so coldhearted.

Her anger mounted as a busy signal came over the line. She waited several seconds, then tried again. This time the phone hardly had time to ring before Mike snatched it up and barked a tense, harried, "Hello!"

"Do you know where Brandon is?" Ashley demanded, plunging right in.

"No. I've been calling all over the neighborhood, asking if anyone has seen him. I was about to call the police—" He broke off. "Ashley? What's going on?"

"That's what I'd like to find out. Did you know Brandon has run away? He showed up at my door with Dawg a little while ago, asking if he could live with me."

"Why would he do a thing like that?"

"I can't believe you really don't know," Ashley replied coldly.

After a long pause Mike said, "I think I'd better come over there so we can get to the bottom of this. As soon as I realized he was missing, I called Mrs. Jackson to come and stay with Sara and Jilly so I can go out and look for him. She should be here any minute. I'll leave as soon as she arrives."

While she waited for Mike to show up, Ashley called Brandon into the kitchen, where she poured him a glass of milk and set a plate of cookies on the table. She also put down a bowl of water and some leftovers from the refrigerator for Dawg. As she moved about the kitchen, Bridget wound around her feet, giving little cries of dismay and darting wary glances at the shaggy intruder who had invaded her domain.

"Now that's no way to treat company," Ashley murmured in a soothing tone. "He's walked a long way, and he's tired and hungry, so be nice to him." As if to illustrate her words, she reached down and patted Dawg's head. As she did so, the bushy tail thumped on the floor.

Brandon chatted amiably as he helped himself to the milk and cookies. It crossed Ashley's mind that he seemed to have made a quick recovery, considering his tearful outburst a little while ago. Before she could examine this curious fact more closely, the doorbell rang.

"Where's Brandon?" Mike asked as soon as Ashley opened the door to him. "Is he all right?"

"He's fine—no thanks to you. I don't see how you can ever look at yourself in a mirror after what you did."

Mike backed away, holding his hands up in front of his chest as if to ward off an attack. "Hey, wait a minute. Just what is it I'm supposed to have done?"

"As if you didn't know," Ashley replied with icy contempt. "How *could* you tell him Dawg had to go to the pound? Why, that's like—like taking Woober away from Jilly."

Mike's brow furrowed into a puzzled frown. "Is that what he told you? That I was going to send Dawg to the pound?" He sounded incredulous.

"Well, didn't you?"

"Of course not. What kind of monster do you think I am?"

"What reason would he have to make up a thing like that?"

"Maybe we'd better have a talk with Brandon and see what he has to say," Mike suggested.

When Ashley went into the kitchen to get Brandon, he was just sliding into his chair. She wondered if he'd been listening to their conversation. "Would you come into the other room?" she said. "Your uncle and I would like to talk to you."

Brandon drained his glass of milk and stuffed one last cookie into his mouth before following Ashley into the living room.

"So—Ashley tells me you're running away because I'm going to send Dawg to the pound," Mike said when Brandon appeared. "That right?"

"That's what you said," Brandon replied, his mouth full of cookie.

"I said nothing of the kind. Why would you make up a story like that?"

"I didn't make it up. When Mrs. Westfall from next door came over today and complained that Dawg had tipped over her garbage can again, you said we were going to have to *do something* about him."

"And you took that to mean I intended to get rid of him?" Mike's tone made it clear he wasn't buying this.

For just a second a wary expression came over Brandon's features, but it was immediately replaced by a look of complete innocence, combined with just a touch of sadness. "But—but I thought that's what you meant."

"I say that at least a couple of times a week. You know as well as I do, all it means is that we're going to have to try harder to keep him out of trouble." Mike sounded as if he were struggling to keep from losing his patience. "Now why did you come to Ashley with such an outlandish story?"

A battle of emotions played over Brandon's face. At last he drew a deep sigh, as if he realized his game—whatever it was—was up. "It wasn't all my idea. Sara and Jilly were in on it too."

"In on what?" Mike demanded. "And I want the truth."

"Well—well, we had to figure out some way to get you and Ashley to talk to each other," Brandon burst out defensively. "We thought if I ran away and came here, then you'd have to come and get me, or Ashley would have to bring me home—"

He broke off as he realized Mike and Ashley were both staring at him, bewildered. It was obvious neither of them had any idea what he was talking about. He rolled his eyes upward and shrugged his shoulders in a gesture of impatience, as if he were wondering how grown-ups could be so dense sometimes. "See, we were watching the other night when Ashley brought Sara home," he explained, "and we saw how she hurried away without even talking to you. And—and that day she brought Woober back to Jilly, *you* didn't wanta talk to *her*. I don't know how you two're ever gonna get together if you both keep acting like that."

"What exactly do you mean—'get together'?" Mike's voice was expressionless.

"Well—*you* know." Clearly he was reluctant to discuss matters of the heart. He seemed aware that he'd gone too far to back down now, though. "We know you like each other—a whole lot," he went on, forging bravely ahead. "We saw how you almost kissed her that day we went to the Space Needle—"

It became quiet enough in the room for its occupants to hear that proverbial pin drop. Ashley could feel herself blushing to the roots of her hair. She found herself fervently wishing she had the power to become invisible.

Mike was the first to break the silence. "So you and your sisters decided to take matters into your own hands?"

Reluctantly Brandon nodded.

"Brandon, you can't just go around arranging people's lives for them."

"But *somebody* had to do *something*," Brandon argued. "Even Mrs. Jackson thinks so."

"Mrs. Jackson?" Mike frowned. "She didn't have anything to do with this, did she?"

"No, but the other night when she shooed us away from the window she said, 'Anyone with half a brain can see those two belong together. I swear, I don't know what they're waiting for.'" Brandon's tone was such a perfect imitation of the housekeeper's forthright, no-nonsense style that Ashley had trouble stifling a smile.

"I think Ashley and I had better have a private discussion," Mike said, his tone giving away nothing of what he was thinking. "Is there anyplace we can be alone?" he asked Ashley.

"Out—out back," she murmured, unsure of what to expect.

"Good. Brandon, you stay here—and see if you can behave yourself," Mike ordered, in a tone that made it clear he was in no mood for any more shenanigans. "Watch television or something. And keep Dawg out of trouble." He took Ashley's arm and briskly steered her out onto the pocket-sized patio outside her back door.

With relief she noted that none of her fellow apartment dwellers seemed to be outside. She was sure that at least a few of them must have witnessed the incident by the pool yesterday afternoon. She wasn't eager to provide further entertainment for her neighbors.

With Mike's hand still on her arm, they strolled out toward the pool area. She was acutely aware of the way the light contact made her skin tingle. Darkness was just starting to fall, and the bright-yellow moon was reflected in the gently rippling water.

"I can hardly believe I was so easily taken in," Ashley commented, embarrassed. "He cried in my arms—*real tears.*"

Mike gave a philosophical shrug. "That kid has a great future either as an actor or a con artist."

Ashley couldn't help laughing at his wry comment. The bit of humor helped take some of the edge off the situation. "Maybe those acting lessons weren't such a good idea. We may have created a monster."

This time it was Mike's turn to laugh. Then his manner turned serious. "You know," he said, stopping and turning to face her, "even though I don't approve of Brandon's methods, I can't help thinking he may be on to something."

"On to something?" Ashley's words came out in a squeak. "What do you mean?"

"The kids have made up their minds we belong

together. Even Mrs. Jackson seems to agree. Maybe it's time we quit fighting it.''

Hesitantly Ashley raised her eyes to his. Just what was he trying to say to her? Hardly daring to breathe, she waited for him to go on.

In the moonlight his gaze captured hers, refusing to let it go. ''We could give it another chance. We had something pretty good going for us in the beginning— until I spoiled everything by getting all hostile that day in the principal's office.''

''It was a perfectly normal reaction. I'm sure it must have seemed as if everyone was ganging up on Brandon—''

He brushed her protests aside. ''I had no right to blame you. It didn't take me long to realize how wrong I was. I wanted to apologize, but then I saw you with that Lattimer character at the Sheldons' party. . . .'' His words trailed off uncertainly. ''There isn't anything between you and that guy, is there?''

''Not a thing,'' she replied with a little smile. ''As a matter of fact, I'd been trying to get that across to him. He couldn't seem to get the idea, but I think that incident yesterday afternoon may have done the trick.''

''Then you're not mad at Dawg for dumping him in the pool?'' Mike asked, sounding relieved.

Ashley's silvery laugh rang out in the moonlight. ''Of course not. I probably owe him a big juicy bone for doing me such a big favor.'' Now it was her turn to look at Mike searchingly. ''What about you and Valerie?''

''I never set eyes on her before that party, and I hope I never see her again. Trying to keep out of her clutches that night was one of the most disagreeable experiences of my life. But why are we wasting time talking about Stewart and Valerie?'' His voice became low and personal. ''It's time to talk about us.''

The way he said *us* sent a thrill of excitement through her. With infinite tenderness he cupped her chin in his hand and tilted her face up to his. As their eyes met, something in his expression made her feel suddenly all warm and weak, as though she were melting inside. Her entire being tingled with the awareness that something cataclysmic was about to happen in her life.

Mike searched her face, as if seeking an answer. ''I love you,'' he said at last. The simple declaration sounded as if it had come from the very depths of his soul.

Shimmering tears blurred Ashley's eyes, but they were tears of happiness. ''I love you too,'' she murmured, her voice breaking.

With a groan Mike pulled her close to him, and she went into his strong, warm embrace willingly. She felt as if she would burst from sheer joy as his lips closed over hers.

When at last they drew apart, he whispered in a voice husky with emotion, ''You have to marry me. I need you. And the kids need you.'' He moved back a step or two so he could look down into her eyes. ''Will you have us?''

''I thought you'd never ask,'' Ashley replied, her lips curving into an impish smile.

At first Mike's expression was incredulous, as if he could hardly believe what he was hearing. Then a look a sheer jubilation came over his features. With a whoop of joy, his hands encircled her waist and he picked her up and swung her around.

"Shhh," Ashley cautioned, her eyes shining and the color high in her cheeks. "What will my neighbors think?"

"They just might think we're in love," Mike replied, setting her down as carefully as if she were made of fragile china.

"And they might be right," she whispered.

All at once Mike's eyes darkened in a way that caused Ashley's pulse to skitter erratically as he took her in his arms again. Everything around them faded away, and for a while they were the only two people in the universe. Mike's lips began a slow, tantalizingly gently exploration from her lips down to the pulsing hollow at the base of her throat. . . .

After a long interval Ashley whispered, "We'd better get back inside and see what Brandon and Dawg are up to."

Mike nodded as he pulled away. "There's no telling what they've done to your apartment by now." Reluctantly they emerged from their own private world and strolled towards Ashley's back door, hand in hand.

Brandon, sitting on the couch, watching television, hardly glanced up. Beneath his attitude of total absorption, Ashley detected an underlying excitement— an air of satisfaction, as if things were working out exactly the way he'd planned. She had a feeling he'd been watching them through the sliding door and had rushed to turn on the television when they'd started back.

Mike touched her arm lightly and nodded toward the

corner of the room, where Dawg was stretched out on the floor. Glancing in the direction he'd indicated, Ashley saw that Bridget was curled up between the two shaggy front paws, purring contentedly.

Leaning close to Ashley, Mike said in a stage whisper, "I think that's a good sign, don't you?"

Ashley nodded, her eyes glowing with happiness.